Elusive Isabel

Jacques Futrelle

Contents

ELUSIVE ISABEL

BY

Jacques Futrelle

TO
THE WONDERFUL WOMAN

I

MISS ISABEL THORNE

All the world rubs elbows in Washington. Outwardly it is merely a city of evasion, of conventionalities, sated with the commonplace pleasures of life, listless, blase even, and always exquisitely, albeit frigidly, courteous; but beneath the still, suave surface strange currents play at cross purposes, intrigue is endless, and the merciless war of diplomacy goes on unceasingly. Occasionally, only occasionally, a bubble comes to the surface, and when it bursts the echo goes crashing around the earth. Sometimes a dynasty is shaken, a nation trembles, a ministry topples over; but the ripple moves and all is placid again. No man may know all that happens there, for then he would be diplomatic master of the world.

"There is plenty of red blood in Washington," remarked a jesting legislative gray-beard, once upon a time, "but it's always frozen before they put it in circulation. Diplomatic negotiations are conducted in the drawing-room, but long before that the fight is fought down cellar. The diplomatists meet at table and there isn't any broken crockery, but you can always tell what the player thinks of the dealer by the way he draws three cards. Everybody is after results; and lots of monarchs of Europe sit up nights polishing their crowns waiting for word from Washington."

So, this is Washington! And here at dinner are the diplomatic representatives of all the nations. That is the British ambassador, that stolid-faced, distinguished-looking, elderly man; and this is the French ambassador, dapper, volatile, plus-correct; here Russia's highest representative wags a huge, blond beard; and yonder is the phlegmatic German ambassador. Scattered around the table, brilliant splotches of color, are the uniformed envoys of the Orient--the smaller the country the more brilliant the splotch. It is a state dinner, to be followed by a state ball, and they are all present.

The Italian ambassador, Count di Rosini, was trying to interpret a French **bon mot** into English for the benefit of the dainty, doll-like wife of the Chinese minister--who was educated at Radcliffe--when a servant leaned over him and laid a sealed envelope beside his plate. The count glanced around at the servant, excused himself to Mrs. Quong Li Wi, and opened the envelope. Inside was a single sheet of embassy note paper, and a terse line signed by his secretary:

"A lady is waiting for you here. She says she must see you immediately, on a matter of the greatest importance."

The count read the note twice, with wrinkled brow, then scribbled on it in pencil:

"Impossible to-night. Tell her to call at the embassy to-morrow morning at half-past ten o'clock."

He folded the note, handed it to the servant, and resumed his conversation with Mrs. Wi.

Half an hour later the same servant placed a second sealed envelope beside his plate. Recognizing the superscription, the ambassador impatiently shoved it aside, intending to disregard it. But irritated curiosity finally triumphed, and he opened it. A white card on which was written this command was his reward:

"It is necessary that you come to the embassy at once."

There was no signature. The handwriting was unmistakably that of a woman, and just as unmistakably strange to him. He frowned a little as he stared at it wonderingly, then idly turned the card over. There was no name on the reverse side--only a crest. Evidently the count recognized this, for his impassive face reflected surprise for an instant, and this was followed by a keen, bewildered interest. Finally he arose, made his apologies, and left the room. His automobile was at the door.

"To the embassy," he directed the chauffeur.

And within five minutes he was there. His secretary met him in the hall.

"The lady is waiting in your office," he explained apologetically. "I gave her your message, but she said she must see you and would write you a line herself. I sent it."

"Quite correct," commented the ambassador. "What name did she give?"

"None," was the reply. "She said none was necessary."

The ambassador laid aside hat and coat and entered his office with a slightly puzzled expression on his face. Standing before a window, gazing idly out into the light-spangled night, was a young woman, rather tall and severely gowned in some rich, glistening stuff which fell away sheerly from her splendid bare shoulders. She turned and he found himself looking into a pair of clear, blue-gray eyes, frank enough and yet in their very frankness possessing an alluring, indefinable subtlety. He would not have called her pretty, yet her smile, slight as it was, was singularly charming, and there radiated from her a something--personality, perhaps--which held his glance. He bowed low, and closed the door.

"I am at your service, Madam," he said in a tone of deep respect. "Please pardon my delay in coming to you."

"It is unfortunate that I didn't write the first note," she apologized graciously. "It would at least have saved a little time. You have the card?"

He produced it silently, crest down, and handed it to her. She struck a match, lighted the card, and it crumbled up in her gloved hand. The last tiny scrap found refuge in a silver tray, where she watched it burn to ashes, then she turned to the ambassador with a brilliant smile. He was still standing.

"The dinner isn't over yet?" she inquired.

"No, Madam, not for another hour, perhaps."

"Then there's no harm done," she went on lightly. "The dinner isn't of any consequence, but I should like very much to attend the ball afterward. Can you arrange it for me?"

"I don't know just how I would proceed, Madam," the ambassador objected diffidently. "It would be rather unusual, difficult, I may say, and--"

"But surely you can arrange it some way?" she interrupted demurely. "The highest diplomatic representative of a great nation should not find it difficult to arrange so simple a matter as--as this?" She was smiling.

"Pardon me for suggesting it, Madam," the ambassador persisted courteously, "but anything out of the usual attracts attention in Washington. I dare say, from the manner of your appearance to-night, that you would not care to attract attention to yourself."

She regarded him with an enigmatic smile.

"I'm afraid you don't know women, Count," she said slowly, at last. "There's nothing dearer to a woman's heart than to attract attention to herself." She laughed--a throaty, silvery note that was charming. "And if you hesitate now, then to-morrow--why, to-morrow I am going to ask that you open to me all this Washington world--this brilliant world of diplomatic society. You see what I ask now is simple."

The ambassador was respectfully silent and deeply thoughtful for a time. There was, perhaps, something of resentment struggling within him, and certainly there was an uneasy feeling of rebellion at this attempt to thrust him forward against all precedent.

"Your requests are of so extraordinary a nature that--" he began in courteous protestation.

There was no trace of impatience in the woman's manner; she was still smiling.

"It is necessary that I attend the ball to-night," she explained, "you may imagine how necessary when I say I sailed from Liverpool six days ago, reaching New York at half-past three o'clock this afternoon; and at half-past four I was on my way here. I have been here less than one hour. I came from Liverpool especially that I might be present; and I even dressed on the train so there would be no delay. Now do you see the necessity of it?"

Diplomatic procedure is along well-oiled grooves, and the diplomatist who steps out of the rut for an instant happens upon strange and unexpected obstacles. Knowing this, the ambassador still hesitated. The woman apparently understood.

"I had hoped that this would not be necessary," she remarked, and she produced a small, sealed envelope. "Please read it."

The ambassador received the envelope with uplifted brows, opened it and read what was written on a folded sheet of paper. Some subtle working of his brain brought a sudden change in the expression of his face. There was wonder in it, and amazement, and more than these. Again he bowed low.

"I am at your service, Madam," he repeated. "I shall take pleasure in making any arrangements that are necessary. Again, I beg your pardon."

"And it will not be so very difficult, after all, will it?" she inquired, and she smiled tauntingly.

"It will not be at all difficult, Madam," the ambassador assured her gravely.

"I shall take steps at once to have an invitation issued to you for to-night; and to-morrow I shall be pleased to proceed as you may suggest."

She nodded. He folded the note, replaced it in the envelope and returned it to her with another deep bow. She drew her skirts about her and sat down; he stood.

"It will be necessary for your name to appear on the invitation," the ambassador went on to explain. "If you will give me your name I'll have my secretary--"

"Oh, yes, my name," she interrupted gaily. "Why, Count, you embarrass me. You know, really, I have no name. Isn't it awkward?"

"I understand perfectly, Madam," responded the count. "I should have said *a* name."

She meditated a moment.

"Well, say--Miss Thorne--Miss Isabel Thorne," she suggested at last. "That will do very nicely, don't you think?"

"Very nicely, Miss Thorne," and the ambassador bowed again. "Please excuse me a moment, and I'll give my secretary instructions how to proceed. There will be a delay of a few minutes."

He opened the door and went out. For a minute or more Miss Thorne sat perfectly still, gazing at the blank wooden panels, then she rose and went to the window again. In the distance, hazy in the soft night, the dome of the capitol rose mistily; over to the right was the congressional library, and out there where the lights sparkled lay Pennsylvania Avenue, a thread of commerce. Miss Thorne saw it all, and suddenly stretched out her arms with an all-enveloping gesture. She stood so for a minute, then they fell beside her, and she was motionless.

Count di Rosini entered.

"Everything is arranged, Miss Thorne," he announced. "Will you go with me in my automobile, or do you prefer to go alone?"

"I'll go alone, please," she answered after a moment. "I shall be there about eleven."

The ambassador bowed himself out.

And so Miss Isabel Thorne came to Washington!

II
MR. CAMPBELL AND THE CABLE

Just as it is one man's business to manufacture watches, and another man's business to peddle shoe-strings, so it was Mr. Campbell's business to know things. He was a human card index, a governmental ready reference posted to the minute and backed by all the tremendous resources of a nation. From the little office in the Secret Service Bureau, where he sat day after day, radiating threads connected with the huge outer world, and enabled him to keep a firm hand on the diplomatic and departmental pulse of Washington. Perhaps he came nearer knowing everything that happened there than any other man living; and no man realized more perfectly than he just how little of all of it he did know.

In person Mr. Campbell was not unlike a retired grocer who had shaken the butter and eggs from his soul and settled back to enjoy a life of placid idleness. He was a little beyond middle age, pleasant of face, white of hair, and blessed with guileless blue eyes. His genius had no sparkle to it; it consisted solely of detail and system and indefatigability, coupled with a memory that was well nigh infallible. His brain was as serene and orderly as a cash register; one almost expected to hear it click.

He sat at his desk intently studying a cable despatch which lay before him. It was in the Secret Service code. Leaning over his shoulder was Mr. Grimm--the Mr. Grimm of the bureau. Mr. Grimm was an utterly different type from his chief. He was younger, perhaps thirty-one or two, physically well proportioned, a little above the average height, with regular features and listless, purposeless eyes--a replica of a hundred other young men who dawdle idly in the windows of their clubs and watch the world hurry by. His manner was languid; his dress showed fastidious care.

Sentence by sentence the bewildering intricacies of the code gave way before the placid understanding of Chief Campbell, and word by word, from the chaos of it, a translation took intelligible form upon a sheet of paper under his right hand. Mr. Grimm, looking on, exhibited only a most perfunctory interest in the extraordinary message he was reading; the listless eyes narrowed a little, that was all. It was a special despatch from Lisbon dated that morning, and signed simply "Gault." Completely translated it ran thus:

"Secret offensive and defensive alliance of the Latin against the English-speaking nations of the world is planned. Italy, France, Spain and two South American republics will soon sign compact in Washington. Proposition just made to Portugal, and may be accepted. Special envoys now working in Mexico and Central and South America. Germany invited to join, but refuses as yet, giving, however, tacit support; attitude of Russia and Japan unknown to me. Prince Benedetto d'Abruzzi, believed to be in Washington at present, has absolute power to sign for Italy, France and Spain. Profound secrecy enjoined and preserved. I learned of it by underground. Shall I inform our minister? Cable instructions."

"So much!" commented Mr. Campbell.

He clasped his hands behind his head, lay back in his chair and sat for a long time, staring with steadfast, thoughtful eyes into the impassive face of his subordinate. Mr. Grimm perched himself on the edge of the desk and with his legs dangling read the despatch a second time, and a third.

"If," he observed slowly, "if any other man than Gault had sent that I should have said he was crazy."

"The peace of the world is in peril, Mr. Grimm," said Campbell impressively, at last. "It had to come, of course, the United States and England against a large part of Europe and all of Central and South America. It had to come, and yet--!"

He broke off abruptly, and picked up the receiver of his desk telephone.

"The White House, please," he requested curtly, and then, after a moment: "Hello! Please ask the president if he will receive Mr. Campbell immediately. Yes, Mr. Campbell of the Secret Service." There was a pause. Mr. Grimm removed his immaculate person from the desk, and took a chair. "Hello! In half an hour? So much!"

The pages of the Almanac de Gotha fluttered through his fingers, and finally he leaned forward and studied a paragraph of it closely. When he raised his eyes again there was that in them which Mr. Grimm had never seen before--a settled, darkening shadow.

"The world-war has long been a chimera, Mr. Grimm," he remarked at last, "but now--now! Think of it! Of course, the Central and South American countries, taken separately, are inconsequential, and that is true, too, of the Latin countries of Europe, except France, but taken in combination, under one directing mind, the allied navies would be--would be formidable, at least. Backed by the moral support of Germany, and perhaps Japan--! Don't you see? Don't you see?"

He lapsed into silence. Mr. Grimm opened his lips to ask a question: Mr. Campbell anticipated it unerringly:

"The purpose of such an alliance? It is not too much to construe it into the first step toward a world-war--a war of reprisal and conquest beside which the other great wars of the world would seem trivial. For the fact has at last come home to the nations of the world that ultimately the English-speaking peoples will dominate it--dominate it, because they are the practical peoples. They have given to the world all its great practical inventions--the railroad, the steamship, electricity, the telegraph and cable--all of them; they are the great civilizing forces, rounding the world up to new moral understanding, for what England has done in Africa and India we have done in a smaller way in the Philippines and Cuba and Porto Rico; they are the great commercial peoples, slowly but surely winning the market-places of the earth; wherever the English or the American flag is planted there the English tongue is being spoken, and there the peoples are being taught the sanity of right living and square dealing.

"It requires no great effort of the imagination, Mr. Grimm, to foresee that day when the traditional power of Paris, and Berlin, and St. Petersburg, and Madrid will be honey-combed by the steady encroachment of our methods. This alliance would indicate that already that day has been foreseen; that there is now a resentment which is about to find expression in one great, desperate struggle for world supremacy. A few hundred years ago Italy--or Rome--was stripped of her power; only recently the United States dispelled the illusion that Spain was anything but a shell; and France--! One can't help but wonder if the power she boasts is not principally on paper. But if their forces are combined? Do you see? It would be an enormous power to reckon with, with a hundred bases of supplies right at our doors."

He rose suddenly and walked over to the window, where he stood for a moment, staring out with unseeing eyes.

"Given a yard of canvas, Mr. Grimm," he went on finally, "a Spanish boy will waste it, a French boy will paint a picture on it, an English boy will built a sail-boat, and an American boy will erect a tent. That fully illustrates the difference in the races."

He abandoned the didactic tone, and returned to the material matter in hand. Mr. Grimm passed him the despatch and he sat down again.

"'Will soon sign compact in Washington,'" he read musingly. "Now I don't know that the signing of that compact can be prevented, but the signing of it on United States soil can be prevented. You will see to that, Mr. Grimm."

"Very well," the young man agreed carelessly. The magnitude of such a task made, apparently, not the slightest impression on him. He languidly drew on his gloves.

"And meanwhile I shall take steps to ascertain the attitude of Russian and Japanese representatives in this city."

Mr. Grimm nodded.

"And now, for Prince Benedetto d'Abruzzi," Mr. Campbell went on slowly. "Officially he is not in Washington, nor the United States, for that matter. Naturally, on such a mission, he would not come as a publicly accredited agent, therefore, I imagine, he is to be sought under another name."

"Of course," Mr. Grimm acquiesced.

"And he would avoid the big hotels."

"Certainly."

Mr. Campbell permitted his guileless blue eyes to linger inquiringly upon those of the young man for half a minute. He caught himself wondering, sometimes, at the perfection of the deliberate indifference with which Mr. Grimm masked his emotions. In his admiration of this quality he quite overlooked the remarkable mask of benevolence behind which he himself hid.

"And the name, D'Abruzzi," he remarked, after a time. "What does it mean to you, Mr. Grimm?"

"It means that I am to deal with a prince of the royal blood of Italy," was the unhesitating response. Mr. Grimm picked up the Almanac de Gotha and glanced at the open page. "Of course, the first thing to do is to find him; the rest will be simple enough." He perused the page carelessly. "I will begin work at once."

III
THE LANGUAGE OF THE FAN

Mr. Grimm was chatting idly with Senorita Rodriguez, daughter of the minister from Venezuela, the while he permitted his listless eyes to wander aimlessly about the spacious ball-room of the German embassy, ablaze with festooned lights, and brilliant with a multi-colored chaos of uniforms. Gleaming pearl-white, translucent in the mass, were the bare shoulders of women; and from far off came the plaintive whine of an orchestra, a pulsing sense rather than a living sound, of music, pointed here and there by the staccato cry of a flute. A zephyr, perfumed with the clean, fresh odor of lilacs, stirred the draperies of the archway which led into the conservatory and rustled the bending branches of palms and ferns.

For a scant instant Mr. Grimm's eyes rested on a young woman who sat a dozen feet away, talking, in playful animation, with an undersecretary of the British embassy--a young woman severely gowned in some glistening stuff which fell away sheerly from her splendid bare shoulders. She glanced up, as if in acknowledgment of his look, and her eyes met his. Frank, blue-gray eyes they were, stirred to their depths now by amusement. She smiled at Senorita Rodriguez, in token of recognition.

"Aren't they wonderful?" asked Senorita Rodriguez with the quick, bubbling enthusiasm of her race.

"What?" asked Mr. Grimm.

"Her eyes," was the reply. "Every person has one dominant feature--with Miss Thorne it is her eyes."

"Miss Thorne?" Mr. Grimm repeated.

"Haven't you met her?" the senorita went on. "Miss Isabel Thorne? She only arrived a few days ago--the night of the state ball. She's my guest at the legation. When an opportunity comes I shall present you to her."

She ran on, about other things, with only an occasional remark from Mr. Grimm, who was thoughtfully nursing his knee. Somewhere through the chatter and effervescent gaiety, mingling with the sound of the pulsing music, he had a singular impression of a rhythmical beat, an indistinct tattoo, noticeable, perhaps, only because of its monotony. After a moment he shot a quick glance at Miss Thorne and understood; it was the tapping of an exquisitely wrought ivory fan against one of her tapering, gloved fingers. She was talking and smiling.

"Dot-dash-dot! Dot-dash-dot! Dot-dash-dot!" said the fan.

Mr. Grimm twisted around in his seat and regaled his listless eyes with a long stare into the senorita's pretty face. Behind the careless ease of repose he was mechanically isolating the faint clatter of the fan.

"Dot-dash-dot! Dot-dash-dot! Dot-dash-dot!"

"Did any one ever accuse you of staring, Mr. Grimm?" demanded the senorita banteringly.

For an instant Mr. Grimm continued to stare, and then his listless eyes swept the ball-room, pausing involuntarily at the scarlet splendor of the minister from Turkey.

"I beg your pardon," he apologized contritely. There was a pause. "The minister from Turkey looks like a barn on fire, doesn't he?"

Senorita Rodriguez laughed, and Mr. Grimm glanced idly toward Miss Thorne. She was still talking, her face alive with interest; and the fan was still tapping rhythmically, steadily, now on the arm of her chair.

"Dot-dash-dot! Dot-dash-dot! Dot-dash-dot! Dot-dash-dot!"

"Pretty women who don't want to be stared at should go with their faces swathed," Mr. Grimm suggested indolently. "Haroun el Raschid there would agree with me on that point, I have no doubt. What a shock he would get if he should happen up at Atlantic City for a week-end in August!"

"Dot-dash-dot! Dot-dash-dot! Dot-dash-dot!"

Mr. Grimm read it with perfect understanding; it was "F--F--F" in the Morse code, the call of one operator to another. Was it accident? Mr. Grimm wondered, and wondering he went on talking lazily:

"Curious, isn't it, the smaller the nation the more color it crowds into the uniforms of its diplomatists? The British ambassador, you will observe, is clothed sanely and modestly, as befits the representative of a great nation; but coming on down by way of Spain and Italy, they get more gorgeous. However, I dare say as stout a heart beats beneath a sky-blue sash as behind the unembellished black of evening dress."

"F--F--F," the fan was calling insistently.

And then the answer came. It took the unexpectedly prosaic form of a violent sneeze, a vociferous outburst on a bench directly behind Mr. Grimm. Senorita Rodriguez jumped, then laughed nervously.

"It startled me," she explained.

"I think there must be a draft from the conservatory," said a man's voice apologetically. "Do you ladies feel it? No? Well, if you'll excuse me--?"

Mr. Grimm glanced back languidly. The speaker was Charles Winthrop Rankin, a brilliant young American lawyer who was attached to the German embassy in an advisory capacity. Among other things he was a Heidelberg man, having spent some dozen years of his life in Germany, where he established influential connections. Mr. Grimm knew him only by sight.

And now the rhythmical tapping of Miss Thorne's fan underwent a change. There was a flutter of gaiety in her voice the while the ivory fan tapped steadily.

"Dot-dot-dot! Dash! Dash-dash-dash! Dot-dot-dash! Dash!"

"S--t--5--u--t," Mr. Grimm read in Morse. He laughed pleasantly at some remark of his companion.

"Dash-dash! Dot-dash! Dash-dot!" said the fan.

"M--a--n," Mr. Grimm spelled it out, the while his listless eyes roved aimlessly over the throng. "S--t--5--u--t m--a--n!" Was it meant for "stout man?" Mr. Grimm wondered.

"Dot-dash-dot! Dot! Dash-dot-dot!"

"F--e--d," that was.

"Dot-dot-dash-dot! Dot-dash! Dash-dot-dash-dot! Dot!"

"Q--a--j--e!" Mr. Grimm was puzzled a little now, but there was not a wrinkle, nor the tiniest indication of perplexity in his face. Instead he began talking of Raphael's cherubs, the remark being called into life by the high complexion of a young man who was passing. Miss Thorne glanced at him once keenly, her splendid eyes fairly aglow, and the fan rattled on in the code.

"Dash-dot! Dot! Dot-dash! Dot-dash-dot!"

"N--e--a--f." Mr. Grimm was still spelling it out.

Then came a perfect jumble. Mr. Grimm followed it with difficulty, a difficulty utterly belied by the quizzical lines about his mouth. As he caught it, it was like this: "J--5--n--s--e--f--v--a--t--5--f," followed by an arbitrary signal which is not in the Morse code: "Dash-dot-dash-dash!"

Mr. Grimm carefully stored that jumble away in some recess of his brain, along with the unknown signal.

"D--5--5--f," he read, and then, on to the end: "B--f--i--n--g 5--v--e--f w--h--e--n g g--5--e--s."

That was all, apparently. The soft clatter of the fan against the arm of the chair ran on meaninglessly after that.

"May I bring you an ice?" Mr. Grimm asked at last.

"If you will, please," responded the senorita, "and when you come back I'll reward you by presenting you to Miss Thorne. You'll find her charming; and Mr. Cadwallader has monopolized her long enough."

Mr. Grimm bowed and left her. He had barely disappeared when Mr. Rankin lounged along in front of Miss Thorne. He glanced at her, paused and greeted her effusively.

"Why, Miss Thorne!" he exclaimed. "I'm delighted to see you here. I understood you would not be present, and--"

Their hands met in a friendly clasp as she rose and moved away, with a nod of excuse to Mr. Cadwallader. A thin slip of paper, thrice folded, passed from Mr. Rankin to her. She tugged at her glove, and thrust the little paper, still folded, inside the palm.

"Is it yes, or no?" Miss Thorne asked in a low tone.

"Frankly, I can't say," was the reply.

"He read the message," she explained hastily, "and now he has gone to decipher it."

She gathered up her trailing skirts over one arm, and together they glided away through the crowd to the strains of a Strauss waltz.

"I'm going to faint in a moment," she said quite calmly to Mr. Rankin. "Please have me sent to the ladies' dressing-room."

"I understand," he replied quietly.

IV
THE FLEEING WOMAN

Mr. Grimm went straight to a quiet nook of the smoking-room and there, after a moment, Mr. Campbell joined him. The bland benevolence of the chief's face was disturbed by the slightest questioning uplift of his brows as he dropped into a seat opposite Mr. Grimm, and lighted a cigar. Mr. Grimm raised his hand, and a servant who stood near, approached them.

"An ice--here," Mr. Grimm directed tersely.

The servant bowed and disappeared, and Mr. Grimm hastily scribbled something on a sheet of paper and handed it to his chief.

"There is a reading, in the Morse code, of a message that seems to be unintelligible," Mr. Grimm explained. "I have reason to believe it is in the Continental code. You know the Continental--I don't."

Mr. Campbell read this:

"St5ut man fed qaje neaf j5nsefvat5f," and then came the unknown, dash-dot-dash-dash. "That," he explained, "is Y in the Continental code." It went on: "d55f bfing 5vef when g g5es."

The chief read it off glibly:

"Stout man, red face, near conservatory door. Bring over when G goes."

"Very well!" commented Mr. Grimm ambiguously.

With no word of explanation, he rose and went out, pausing at the door to take the ice which the servant was bringing in. The seat where he had left Senorita Rodriguez was vacant; so was the chair where Miss Thorne had been. He glanced about inquiringly, and a servant who stood stolidly near the conservatory door approached him.

"Pardon, sir, but the lady who was sitting here," and he indicated the chair where Miss Thorne had been sitting, "fainted while dancing, and the lady who was with you went along when she was removed to the ladies' dressing-room, sir."

Mr. Grimm's teeth closed with a little snap.

"Did you happen to notice any time this evening a stout gentleman, with red face, near the conservatory door?" he asked.

The servant pondered a moment, then shook his head.

"No, sir."

"Thank you."

Mr. Grimm was just turning away, when there came the sharp, vibrant cra-a-sh! of a revolver, somewhere off to his left. The president! That was his first thought. One glance across the room to where the chief executive stood, in conversation with two other gentlemen, reassured him. The choleric blue eyes of the president had opened a little at the sound, then he calmly resumed the conversation. Mr. Grimm impulsively started toward the little group, but already a cordon was being drawn there--a cordon of quiet-faced, keen-eyed men, unobstrusively forcing their way through the crowd. There was Johnson, and Hastings, and Blair, and half a dozen others.

The room had been struck dumb. The dancers stopped, with tense, inquiring looks, and the plaintive whine of the orchestra, far away, faltered, then ceased. There was one brief instant of utter silence in which white-faced women clung to the arms of their escorts, and the brilliant galaxy of colors halted. Then, after a moment, there came clearly through the stillness, the excited, guttural command of the German ambassador.

"Keep on blaying, you tam fools! Keep on blaying!"

The orchestra started again tremulously. Mr. Grimm nodded a silent approval of the ambassador's command, then turned away toward his left, in the direction of the shot. After the first dismay, there was a general movement of the crowd in that direction, a movement which was checked by Mr. Campbell's appearance upon a chair, with a smile on his bland face.

"No harm done," he called. "One of the officers present dropped his revolver, and it was accidently discharged. No harm done."

There was a moment's excited chatter, deep-drawn breaths of relief, the orchestra swung again into the interrupted rhythm, and the dancers moved on. Mr. Grimm went straight to his chief, who had stepped down from the chair. Two other Secret Service men stood behind him, blocking the doorway that opened into a narrow hall.

"This way," directed the chief tersely.

Mr. Grimm walked along beside him. They skirted the end of the ball-room until they came to another door opening into the hall. Chief Campbell pushed it open, and entered. One of his men stood just inside.

"What was it, Gray?" asked the chief.

"Senor Alvarez, of the Mexican legation, was shot," was the reply.

"Dead?"

"Only wounded. He's in that room," and he indicated a door a little way down the hall. "Fairchild, two servants, and a physician are with him."

"Who shot him?"

"Don't know. We found him lying in the hall here."

Still followed by Mr. Grimm, the chief entered the room, and together they bent over the wounded man. The bullet had entered the torso just below the ribs on the left side.

"It's a clean wound," the physician was explaining. "The bullet passed through. There's no immediate danger."

Senor Alvarez opened his eyes, and stared about him in bewilderment; then alarm overspread his face, and he made spasmodic efforts to reach the inside breast pocket of his coat. Mr. Grimm obligingly thrust his hand into the pocket and drew out its contents, the while Senor Alvarez struggled frantically.

"Just a moment," Mr. Grimm advised quietly. "I'm only going to let you see if it is here. Is it?"

He held the papers, one by one, in front of the wounded man, and each time a shake of the head was his answer. At the last Senor Alvarez closed his eyes again.

"What sort of paper was it?" inquired Mr. Grimm.

"None of your business," came the curt answer.

"Who shot you?"

"None of your business."

"A man?"

Senor Alvarez was silent.

"A woman?"

Still silence.

With some new idea Mr. Grimm turned away suddenly and started out into the hall. He met a maid-servant at the door, coming in. Her face was blanched, and she stuttered through sheer excitement.

"A lady, sir--a lady--" she began babblingly.

Mr. Grimm calmly closed the door, shutting in the wounded man, Chief Campbell and the others. Then he caught the maid sharply by the arm and shook some coherence into her disordered brain.

"A lady--she ran away, sir," the girl went on, in blank surprise.

"What lady?" demanded Mr. Grimm coldly. "Where did she run from? Why did she run?" The maid stared at him with mouth agape. "Begin at the beginning."

"I was in that room, farther down the hall, sir," the maid explained. "The door was open. I heard the shot, and it frightened me so--I don't know--I was afraid to look out right away, sir. Then, an instant later, a lady come running along the hall, sir--that way," and she indicated the rear of the house. "Then I came to the door and looked out to see who it was, and what was the matter, sir. I was standing there when a man--a man came along after the lady, and banged the door in my face, sir. The door had a spring lock, and I was so--so frightened and excited I couldn't open it right away, sir, and--and when I did I came here to see what was the matter." She drew a deep breath and stopped.

"That all?" demanded Mr. Grimm.

"Yes, sir, except--except the lady had a pistol in her hand, sir--"

Mr. Grimm regarded her in silence for a moment.

"Who was the lady?" he asked at last.

"I forget her name, sir. She was the lady who--who fainted in the ball-room, sir, just a few minutes ago."

Whatever emotion may have been aroused within Mr. Grimm it certainly found no expression in his face. When he spoke again his voice was quite calm.

"Miss Thorne, perhaps?"

"Yes, sir, that's the name--Miss Thorne. I was in the ladies' dressing-room when she was brought in, sir, and I remember some one called her name."

Mr. Grimm took the girl, still a-quiver with excitement, and led her along the hall to where Gray stood.

"Take this girl in charge, Gray," he directed. "Lock her up, if necessary. Don't permit her to say one word to anybody--anybody you understand, except the chief."

Mr. Grimm left them there. He passed along the hall, glancing in each room as he went, until he came to a short flight of stairs leading toward the kitchen. He went on down silently. The lights were burning, but the place was still, deserted. All the servants who belonged there were evidently, for the moment, transferred to other posts. He passed on through the kitchen and out the back door into the street.

A little distance away, leaning against a lamp-post, a man was standing. He might have been waiting for a car. Mr. Grimm approached him.

"Beg pardon," he said, "did you see a woman come out of the back door, there?"

"Yes, just a moment or so ago," replied the stranger. "She got into an automobile at the corner. I imagine this is hers," and he extended a handkerchief, a dainty, perfumed trifle of lace. "I picked it up immediately after she passed."

Mr. Grimm took the handkerchief and examined it under the light. For a time he was thoughtful, with lowered eyes, which, finally raised, met those of the stranger with a scrutinizing stare.

"Why," asked Mr. Grimm slowly and distinctly, "why did you slam the door in the girl's face?"

"Why did I--what?" came the answering question.

"Why did you slam the door in the girl's face?" Mr. Grimm repeated slowly.

The stranger stared in utter amazement--an amazement so frank, so unacted, so genuine, that Mr. Grimm was satisfied.

"Did you see a man come out the door?" Mr. Grimm pursued.

"No. Say, young fellow, I guess you've had a little too much to drink, haven't you?"

But by that time Mr. Grimm was turning the corner.

V
A VISIT TO THE COUNT

The bland serenity of Mr. Campbell's face was disturbed by thin, spidery lines of perplexity, and the guileless blue eyes were vacant as he stared at the top of his desk. Mr. Grimm was talking.

"From the moment Miss Thorne turned the corner I lost all trace of her," he said. "Either she had an automobile in waiting, or else she was lucky enough to find one immediately she came out. She did not return to the embassy ball last night--that much is certain." He paused reflectively. "She is a guest of Senorita Inez Rodriguez at the Venezuelan legation," he added.

"Yes, I know," his chief nodded.

"I didn't attempt to see her there last night for two reasons," Mr. Grimm continued. "First, she can have no possible knowledge of the fact that she is suspected, unless perhaps the man who slammed the door--" He paused. "Anyway, she will not attempt to leave Washington; I am confident of that. Again, it didn't seem wise to me to employ the ordinary crude police methods in the case--that is, go to the Venezuelan legation and kick up a row."

For a long time Campbell was silent; the perplexed lines still furrowed his benevolent forehead.

"The president is very anxious that we get to facts in this reported Latin alliance as soon as possible," he said at last, irrelevantly. "He mentioned the matter last night, and he has been keeping in constant communication with Gault, in Lisbon, who, however, has not been able to add materially to the original despatch. Under all the circumstances don't you think it would be best for me to relieve you of the investigation of this shooting affair so that you can concentrate on this greater and more important thing?"

"Will Senor Alvarez die?" asked Mr. Grimm in turn.

"His condition is serious, although the wound is not necessarily fatal," was the reply.

Mr. Grimm arose, stretched his long legs and stood for a little while gazing out the window. Finally he turned to his chief:

"What do we know, here in the bureau, about Miss Thorne?"

"Thus far the reports on her are of the usual perfunctory nature," Mr. Campbell explained. He drew a card from a pigeonhole of his desk and glanced at it. "She arrived in Washington two weeks and two days ago from New York, off the *Lusitania*, from Liverpool. She brought some sort of an introduction to Count di Rosini, the Italian ambassador, and he obtained for her a special invitation to the state ball, which was held that night. Until four days ago she was a guest at the Italian embassy, but now, as you know, is a guest at the Venezuelan legation. Since her arrival here she has been prominently pushed forward into society; she has gone everywhere, and been received everywhere in the diplomatic set. We have no knowledge of her beyond this."

There was a question in Mr. Grimm's listless eyes as they met those of his chief. The same line of thought was running in both their minds, born, perhaps, of the association of ideas--Italy as one of three great nations known to be in the Latin compact; Prince Benedetto d'Abruzzi, of Italy, the secret envoy of three countries; the sudden appearance of Miss Thorne at the Italian embassy. And in the mind of the younger man there was more than this--a definite knowledge of a message cunningly transmitted to Mr. Rankin, of the German embassy, by Miss Thorne there in the ball-room.

"Can you imagine--" he asked slowly, "can you imagine a person who would be of more value to the Latin governments in Washington right at this stage of the negotiations than a brilliant woman agent?"

"I most certainly can not," was the chief's unhesitating response.

"In that case I *don't* think it would be wise to transfer the investigation of the shooting affair to another man," said Mr. Grimm emphatically, reverting to his chief's question. "I think, on the contrary, we should find out more about Miss Thorne."

"Precisely," Campbell agreed.

"Ask all the great capitals about her--Madrid, Paris and Rome, particularly; then, perhaps, London and Berlin and St. Petersburg."

Mr. Campbell thoughtfully scribbled the names of the cities on a slip of paper.

"Do you intend to arrest Miss Thorne for the shooting?" he queried.

"I don't know," replied Mr. Grimm frankly. "I don't know," he repeated musingly. "If I *do* arrest her immediately I may cut off a clue which will lead to the other affair. I don't know," he concluded.

"Use your own judgment, and bear in mind that a man--a man slammed the door in the maid's face."

"I shall not forget him," Mr. Grimm answered. "Now I'm going over to talk to Count di Rosini for a while."

The young man went out, thoughtfully tugging at his gloves. The Italian ambassador received him with an inquiring uplift of his dark brows.

"I came to make some inquiries in regard to Miss Thorne--Miss Isabel Thorne," Mr. Grimm informed him frankly.

The count was surprised, but it didn't appear in his face.

"As I understand it," the young man pursued, "you are sponsor for her in Washington?"

The count, evasively diplomatic, born and bred in a school of caution, considered the question from every standpoint.

"It may be that I am so regarded," he admitted at last.

"May I inquire if the sponsorship is official, personal, social, or all three?" Mr. Grimm continued.

There was silence for a long time.

"I don't see the trend of your questioning," said the ambassador finally. "Miss Thorne is worthy of my protection in every way."

"Let's suppose a case," suggested Mr. Grimm blandly. "Suppose Miss Thorne had--had, let us say, shot a man, and he was about to die, would you feel justified in withdrawing that--that protection, as you call it?"

"Such a thing is preposterous!" exclaimed the ambassador. "The utter absurdity of such a charge would impel me to offer her every assistance."

Mr. Grimm nodded.

"And if it were proved to your satisfaction that she *did* shoot him?" he went on evenly.

The count's lips were drawn together in a straight line.

"Whom, may I ask," he inquired frigidly, "are we supposing that Miss Thorne shot?"

"No one, particularly," Mr. Grimm assured him easily. "Just suppose that she *had* shot anybody--me, say, or Senor Alvarez?"

"I can't answer a question so ridiculous as that."

"And suppose we go a little further," Mr. Grimm insisted pleasantly, "and assume that you *knew* she *had* shot some one, say Senor Alvarez, and you *could* protect her from the consequences, *would* you?"

"I decline to suppose anything so utterly absurd," was the rejoinder.

Mr. Grimm sat with his elbows on his knees, idly twisting a seal ring on his little finger. The searching eyes of the ambassador found his face blankly inscrutable.

"Diplomatic representatives in Washington have certain obligations to this government," the young man reminded him. "We--that is, the government of the United States--undertake to guarantee the personal safety of every accredited representative; in return for that protection we must insist upon the name and identity of a dangerous person who may be known to any foreign representative. Understand, please, I'm not asserting that Miss Thorne is a dangerous person. You are sponsor for her here. Is she, in every way, worthy of your protection?"

"Yes," said the ambassador flatly.

"I can take it, then, that the introduction she brought to you is from a person whose position is high enough to insure Miss Thorne's position?"

"That is correct."

"Very well!"

And Mr. Grimm went away.

VI
REVELATIONS

Some vague, indefinable shadow darkened Miss Thorne's clear, blue-gray eyes, in sharp contrast to the glow of radiant health in her cheeks, as she stepped from an automobile in front of the Venezuelan legation, and ran lightly up the steps. A liveried servant opened the door.

"A gentleman is waiting for you, Madam," he announced. "His card is here on the--"

"I was expecting him," she interrupted.

"Which room, please?"

"The blue room, Madam."

Miss Thorne passed along the hallway which led to a suite of small drawing-rooms opening on a garden in the rear, pushed aside the portieres, and entered.

"I'm sorry I've kept you--" she began, and then, in a tone of surprise: "I beg your pardon."

A gentleman rose and bowed gravely.

"I am Mr. Grimm of the Secret Service," he informed her with frank courtesy. "I am afraid you were expecting some one else; I handed my card to the footman."

For an instant the blue-gray eyes opened wide in astonishment, and then some quick, subtle change swept over Miss Thorne's face. She smiled graciously and motioned him to a seat.

"This is quite a different meeting from the one Senorita Rodriguez had planned, isn't it?" she asked.

There was a taunting curve on her scarlet lips; the shadow passed from her eyes; her slim, white hands lay idle in her lap. Mr. Grimm regarded her reflectively. There was a determination of steel back of this charming exterior; there was an indomitable will, a keen brain, and all of a woman's intuition to reckon with. She was silent, with a questioning upward slant of her arched brows.

"I am not mistaken in assuming that you are a secret agent of the Italian government, am I?" he queried finally.

"No," she responded readily.

"In that event I may speak with perfect frankness?" he went on. "It would be as useless as it would be absurd to approach the matter in any other manner?" It was a question.

Miss Thorne was still smiling, but again the vague, indefinable shadow, momentarily lifted, darkened her eyes.

"You may be frank, of course," she said pleasantly. "Please go on."

"Senor Alvarez was shot at the German Embassy Ball last night," Mr. Grimm told her.

Miss Thorne nodded, as if in wonder.

"Did you, or did you not, shoot him?"

It was quite casual. She received the question without change of countenance, but involuntarily she caught her breath. It might have been a sigh of relief.

"Why do you come to me with such a query?" she asked in turn.

"I beg your pardon," interposed Mr. Grimm steadily. "Did you, or did you not, shoot him?"

"No, of course I didn't shoot him," was the reply. If there was any emotion in the tone it was merely impatience. "Why do you come to me?" she repeated.

"Why do I come to you?" Mr. Grimm echoed the question, while his listless eyes rested on her face. "I will be absolutely frank, as I feel sure you would be under the same circumstances." He paused a moment; she nodded. "Well, immediately after the shooting you ran along the hallway with a revolver in your hand; you ran down the steps into the kitchen, and out through the back door, where you entered an automobile. That is not conjecture; it is susceptible of proof by eye witnesses."

Miss Thorne rose suddenly with a queer, helpless little gesture of her arms, and walked to the window. She stood there for a long time with her hands clasped behind her back.

"That brings us to another question," Mr. Grimm continued mercilessly. "If you did not shoot Senor Alvarez, do you know who did?"

There was another long pause.

"I want to believe you, Miss Thorne," he supplemented.

She turned quickly with something of defiance in her attitude.

"Yes, I know," she said slowly. "It were useless to deny it."

"Who was it?"

"I won't tell you."

Mr. Grimm leaned forward in his chair, and spoke earnestly.

"Understand, please, that by that answer you assume equal guilt with the person who actually did the shooting," he explained. "If you adhere to it you compel me to regard you as an accomplice." His questioning took a different line.

"Will you explain how the revolver came into your possession?"

"Oh, I--I picked it up in the hallway there," she replied vaguely.

"I want to believe you, Miss Thorne," Mr. Grimm said again.

"You may. I picked it up in the hallway," she repeated. "I saw it lying there and picked it up."

"Why that, instead of giving an alarm?"

"No alarm was necessary. The shot itself was an alarm."

"Then why," Mr. Grimm persisted coldly, "did you run along the hallway and escape by way of the kitchen? If you did not do the shooting, why the necessity of escape, carrying the revolver?"

There was that in the blue-gray eyes which brought Mr. Grimm to his feet. His hands gripped each other cruelly; his tone was calm as always.

"Why did you take the revolver?" he asked.

Miss Thorne's head drooped forward a little, and she was silent.

"There are only two possibilities, of course," he went on. "First, that you, in spite of your denial, did the shooting."

"I did not!" The words fairly burst from her tightly closed lips.

"Or that you knew the revolver, and took it to save the person, man or woman, who fired the shot. I will assume, for the moment, that this is correct. Where is the revolver?"

From the adjoining room there came a slight noise, a faint breath of sound; or it might have been only an echo of silence. Their eyes were fixed each upon the others unwaveringly, with not a flicker to indicate that either had heard. After a moment Miss Thorne returned to her chair and sat down.

"It's rather a singular situation, isn't it, Mr. Grimm?" she inquired irrelevantly. "You, Mr. Grimm of the Secret Service of the United States; I, Isabel Thorne, a secret agent of Italy together here, one accusing the other of a crime, and perhaps with good reason."

"Where is the revolver?" Mr. Grimm insisted.

"If you were any one else *but* you! I could not afford to be frank with you and--"

"If you had been any one else but *you* I should have placed you under arrest when I entered the room."

She smiled, and inclined her head.

"I understand," she said pleasantly. "For the reason that you are Mr. Grimm of the Secret Service I shall tell you the truth. I *did* take the revolver because I knew who had fired the shot. Believe me when I tell you that that person did not act with my knowledge or consent. You do believe that? You do?" She was pleading, eager to convince him.

After a while Mr. Grimm nodded.

"The revolver is beyond your reach and shall remain so," she resumed. "According to your laws I suppose I am an accomplice. That is my misfortune. It will in no way alter my determination to keep silent. If I am arrested I can't help it." She studied his face with hopeful eyes. "Am I to be arrested?"

"Where is the paper that was taken from Senor Alvarez immediately after he was shot?" Mr. Grimm queried.

"I don't know," she replied frankly.

"As I understand it, then, the motive for the shooting was to obtain possession of that paper? For your government?"

"The individual who shot Senor Alvarez *did* obtain the paper, yes. And now, please, am I to be arrested?"

"And just what was the purpose, may I inquire, of the message you telegraphed with your fan in the ball-room?"

"You read that?" exclaimed Miss Thorne in mock astonishment. "You read that?"

"And the man who read that message? Perhaps he shot the senor?"

"Perhaps," she taunted.

For a long time Mr. Grimm stood staring at her, staring, staring. She, too, rose, and faced him quietly.

"Am I to be arrested?" she asked again.

"Why do you make me do it?" he demanded.

"That is my affair."

Mr. Grimm laid a hand upon her arm, a hand that had never known nervousness. A moment longer he stared, and then:

"Madam, you are my prisoner for the attempted murder of Senor Alvarez!"

The rings on the portieres behind him clicked sharply, and the draperies parted. Mr. Grimm stood motionless, with his hand on Miss Thorne's arm.

"You were inquiring a moment ago for a revolver," came in a man's voice. "Here it is!"

Mr. Grimm found himself inspecting the weapon from the barrel end. After a moment his glance shifted to the blazing eyes of the man who held it--a young man, rather slight, with clean-cut, aristocratic features, and of the pronounced Italian type.

"My God!" The words came from Miss Thorne's lips almost in a scream. "Don't--!"

"I did make some inquiries about a revolver, yes," Mr. Grimm interrupted quietly. "Is this the one?"

He raised his hand quite casually, and his fingers closed like steel around the weapon. Behind his back Miss Thorne made some quick emphatic gesture, and the new-comer released the revolver.

"I shall ask you, please, to free Miss Thorne," he requested courteously. "I shot Senor Alvarez. I, too, am a secret agent of the Italian government, willing and able to defend myself. Miss Thorne has told you the truth; she had nothing whatever to do with it. She took the weapon and escaped because it was mine. Here is the paper that was taken from Senor Alvarez," and he offered a sealed envelope. "I have read it; it is not what I expected. You may return it to Senor Alvarez with my compliments."

After a moment Mr. Grimm's hand fell away from Miss Thorne's arm, and he regarded the new-comer with an interest in which admiration, even, played a part.

"Your name?" he asked finally.

"Pietro Petrozinni," was the ready reply. "As I say, I accept all responsibility."

A few minutes later Mr. Grimm and his prisoner passed out of the legation side by side, and strolled down the street together, in amicable conversation. Half an hour later Senor Alvarez identified Pietro Petrozinni as the man who shot him; and the maid servant expressed a belief that he was the man who slammed the door in her face.

VII
THE SIGNAL

A nd the original question remains unanswered," remarked Mr. Campbell.

"The original question?" repeated Mr. Grimm.

"Where is Prince Benedetto d'Abruzzi, the secret envoy?" his chief reminded him.

"I wonder!" mused the young man.

"If the Latin compact is signed in the United States--?"

"The Latin compact will *not* be signed in the United States," Mr. Grimm interrupted. And then, after a moment: "Have we received any further reports on Miss Thorne? I mean reports from our foreign agents?"

The chief shook his head.

"Inevitably, by some act or word, she will lead us to the prince," declared Mr. Grimm, "and the moment he is known to us everything becomes plain sailing. We know she *is* a secret agent--I expected a denial, but she was quite frank about it. And I had no intention whatever of placing her under arrest. I knew some one was in the adjoining room because of a slight noise in there, and I knew she knew it. She raised her voice a little, obviously for the benefit of whoever was there. From that point everything I said and did was to compel that person, whoever it was, to show himself."

His chief nodded, understandingly. Mr. Grimm was silent for a little, then went on:

"The last possibility in my mind at that moment," he confessed, "was that the person in there was the man who shot Senor Alvarez. Frankly I had half an idea that--that it might be the prince in person." Suddenly his mood changed: "And now our lady of mystery may come and go as she likes because I know, even if a dozen of our men have ransacked Washington in vain for the prince, she will inevitably lead us to him. And that reminds me: I should like to borrow Blair, and Hastings, and Johnson. Please plant them so they may keep constant watch on Miss Thorne. Let them report to you, and, wherever I am, I will reach you over the 'phone."

"By the way, what was in that sealed packet that was taken from Senor Alvarez?" Campbell inquired curiously.

"It had something to do with some railroad franchises," responded Mr. Grimm as he rose. "I sealed it again and returned it to the senor. Evidently it was not what Signor Petrozinni expected to find--in fact, he admitted it wasn't what he was looking for."

For a little while the two men gazed thoughtfully, each into the eyes of the other, then Mr. Grimm entered his private office where he sat for an hour with his immaculate boots on his desk, thinking. A world-war--he had been thrust forward by his government to prevent it--subtle blue-gray eyes--his Highness, Prince Benedetto d'Abruzzi--a haunting smile and scarlet lips.

At about the moment he rose to go out, Miss Thorne, closely veiled, left the Venezuelan legation and walked rapidly down the street to a corner, where, without a word, she entered a waiting automobile. The wheels spun and the car leaped forward. For a mile or more it wound aimlessly in and out, occasionally bisecting its own path; finally Miss Thorne leaned forward and touched the chauffeur on the arm.

"Now!" she said.

The car straightened out into a street of stately residences and scuttled along until the placid bosom of the Potomac came into view; beside that for a few minutes, then over the bridge to the Virginia side, in the dilapidated little city of Alexandria. The car did not slacken its speed, but wound in and out through dingy streets, past tumble-down negro huts, for half an hour before it came to a standstill in front of an old brick mansion.

"This is number ninety-seven," the chauffeur announced.

Miss Thorne entered the house with a key and was gone for ten minutes, perhaps. She was readjusting her veil when she came out and stepped into the car silently. Again it moved forward, on to the end of the dingy street, and finally into the open country. Three, four, five miles, perhaps, out the old Baltimore Road, and again the car stopped, this time in front of an ancient colonial farm-house.

Outwardly the place seemed to be deserted. The blinds, battered and stripped of paint by wind and rain, were all closed, and one corner of the small veranda had crumbled away from age and neglect. A narrow path, strewn with pine needles, led tortuously up to the door. In the rear of the house, rising from an old barn, a thin pole with a cup-like attachment at the apex, thrust its point into the open above the dense, odorous pines. It appeared to be a wireless mast. Miss Thorne passed around the house, and entered the barn.

A man came forward and kissed her--a thin, little man of indeterminate age--drying his hands on a piece of cotton waste. His face was pale with the pallor of one who knows little outdoor life, his eyes deep-set and a-glitter with some feverish inward fire, and the thin lips were pressed together in a sharp line. Behind him was a long bench on which were scattered tools of various sorts, fantastically shaped chemical apparatus, two or three electric batteries of odd sizes, and ranged along one end of it, in a row, were a score or more metal spheroids, a shade larger than a one-pound shell. From somewhere in the rear came the clatter of a small gasoline engine, and still farther away was an electric dynamo.

"Is the test arranged, Rosa?" the little man queried eagerly in Italian.

"The date is not fixed yet," she replied in the same language. "It will be, I hope, within the next two weeks. And then--"

"Fame and fortune for both of us," he interrupted with quick enthusiasm. "Ah, Rosa, I have worked and waited so long for this, and now it will come, and with it the dominion of the world again by our country. How will I know when the date is fixed? It would not be well to write me here."

My lady of mystery stroked the slender, nervous hand caressingly, and a great affection shone in the blue-gray eyes.

"At eight o'clock on the night of the test," she explained, still speaking Italian, "a single light will appear at the apex of the capitol dome in Washington. That is the signal agreed upon; it can be seen by all in the city, and is visible here from the window of your bedroom."

"Yes, yes," he exclaimed. The feverish glitter in his eyes deepened.

"If there is a fog, of course you will not attempt the test," she went on.

"No, not in a fog," he put in quickly. "It must be clear."

"And if it is clear you can see the light in the dome without difficulty."

"And all your plans are working out well?"

"Yes. And yours?"

"I don't think there is any question but that both England and the United States will buy. Do you know what it means? Do you know what it means?" He was silent a moment, his hands working nervously. Then, with an effort: "And his Highness?"

"His Highness is safe." The subtle eyes grew misty, thoughtful for a moment, then cleared again. "He is safe," she repeated.

"Mexico and Venezuela were--?" he began.

"We don't know, yet, what they will do. The Venezuelan answer is locked in the safe at the legation; I will know what it is within forty-eight hours." She was silent a little. "Our difficulty now, our greatest difficulty, is the hostility of the French ambassador to the compact. His government has not yet notified him of the presence of Prince d'Abruzzi; he does not believe in the feasibility of the plan, and we have to--to proceed to extremes to prevent him working against us."

"But they *must* see the incalculable advantages to follow upon such a compact, with the vast power that will be given to them over the whole earth by this." He indicated the long, littered work-table. "They *must* see it."

"They will see it, Luigi," said Miss Thorne gently. "And now, how are you? Are you well? Are you comfortable? It's such a dreary old place here."

"I suppose so," he replied, and he met the solicitous blue-gray eyes for an instant. "Yes, I am quite comfortable," he added. "I have no time to be otherwise with all the work I must do. It will mean so much!"

They were both silent for a time. Finally Miss Thorne walked over to the long table and curiously lifted one of the spheroids. It was a sinister looking thing, nickeled, glittering. At one end of it was a delicate, vibratory apparatus, not unlike the transmitter of a telephone, and the other end was threaded, as if the spheroid was made as an attachment to some other device.

"With that we control the world!" exclaimed the man triumphantly. "And it's mine, Rosa, mine!"

"It's wonderful!" she mused softly. "Wonderful! And now I must go. I may not see you again until after the test, because I shall be watched and followed wherever

I go. If I get an opportunity I shall reach you by telephone, but not even that unless it is necessary. There is always danger, always danger!" she repeated thoughtfully. She was thinking of Mr. Grimm.

"I understand," said the man simply.

"And look out for the signal--the light in the apex of the capitol dome," she went on. "I understand the night must be perfectly clear; and *you* understand that the test is to be made promptly at three o'clock by your chronometer?"

"At three o'clock," he repeated.

For a moment they stood with their arms around each other, then tenderly his visitor kissed him, and went out. He remained looking after her vacantly until the chug-chug of her automobile, as it moved off down the road, was lost in the distance, then turned again to the long work-table.

VIII
MISS THORNE AND NOT MISS THORNE

From a pleasant, wide-open bay-window of her apartments on the second floor, Miss Thorne looked out upon the avenue with inscrutable eyes. Behind the closely drawn shutters of another bay-window, farther down the avenue, on the corner, she knew a man named Hastings was hiding; she knew that for an hour or more he had been watching her as she wrote. In the other direction, in a house near the corner, another man named Blair was similarly ensconced, and he, too, had been watching as she wrote. There should be a third man, Johnson. Miss Thorne curiously studied the face of each passer-by, seeking therein something to remember.

She sat at the little mahogany desk and a note with the ink yet wet upon it lay face up before her. It was addressed to Signor Pietro Petrozinni in the district prison, and read:

"My Dear Friend:

"I have been waiting to write you with the hope that I could report Senor Alvarez out of danger, but his condition, I regret to say, remains unchanged. Shall I send an attorney to you? Would you like a book of any kind? Or some delicacy sent in from a restaurant? Can I be of any service to you in any way? If I can please drop me a line.

"Sincerely,

"Isabel Thorne."

At last she rose and standing in the window read the note over, folded it, placed it in an envelope and sealed it. A maid came in answer to her ring, and there at the window, under the watchful eyes of Blair and Hastings--and, perhaps, Johnson--she handed the note to the maid with instructions to mail it immediately. Two minutes later she saw the maid go out along the avenue to a post-box on the corner.

Then she drew back into the shadow of the room, slipped on a dark-colored wrap, and, standing away from the window, safe beyond the reach of prying eyes, waited patiently for the postman. He appeared about five o'clock and simultaneously another man turned the corner near the post-box and spoke to him. Then, together, they disappeared from view around the corner.

"So that's Johnson, is it?" mused Miss Thorne, and she smiled a little. "Mr. Grimm certainly pays me the compliment of having me carefully watched."

A few minutes later she dropped into the seat at the desk again. The dark wrap had been thrown aside and Hastings and Blair from their hiding-places could see her distinctly. After a while they saw her rise quickly, as an automobile turned into the avenue, and lean toward the window eagerly looking out. The car came to a standstill in front of the legation, and Mr. Cadwallader, an under-secretary of the British embassy, who was alone in the car, raised his cap. She nodded and smiled, then disappeared in the shadows of the room again.

Mr. Cadwallader went to the door, spoke to the servant there, then returned and busied himself about the car. Hastings and Blair watched intently both the door and the window for a long time; finally a closely veiled and muffled figure appeared at the bay-window, and waved a gloved hand at Mr. Cadwallader, who again lifted his cap. A minute later the veiled woman came out of the front door, shook hands with Mr. Cadwallader, and got in the car. He also climbed in, and the car moved slowly away.

Simultaneously the front door of the house on the corner, where Hastings had been hiding, and the front door of the house near the corner, where Blair had been hiding, opened and two heads peered out. As the car approached Hastings' hiding-place he withdrew into the hallway; but Blair came out and hurried past the legation in the direction of the rapidly disappearing motor. Hastings joined him; they spoke together, then turned the corner.

It was about ten o'clock that night when Hastings reported to Mr. Campbell at his home.

"We followed the car in a rented automobile from the time it turned the corner, out through Alexandria, and along the old Baltimore Road into the city of Baltimore," he explained. "It was dark by the time we reached Alexandria, but we stuck to the car ahead, running without lights until we came in sight of Druid Hill Park, and then we had to show lights or be held up. We covered those forty miles going in less than two hours.

"After the car passed Druid Hill it slowed up a little, and ran off the turnpike into North Avenue, then into North Charles Street, and slowly along that as if they were looking for a number. At last it stopped and Miss Thorne got out and entered a house. She was gone for more than half an hour, leaving Mr. Cadwallader with the car. While she was gone I made some inquiries and learned that the house was occupied by a Mr. Thomas Q. Griswold. I don't know anything else about him; Blair may have learned something.

"Now comes the curious part of it," and Hastings looked a little sheepish. "When Miss Thorne came out of the house she was not Miss Thorne at all--she was Senorita Inez Rodriguez, daughter of the Venezuelan minister. She wore the same clothing Miss Thorne had worn going, but her veil was lifted. Veiled and all muffled up one would have taken oath it was the same woman. She and Cadwallader are back in Washington now, or are coming. That's all, except Blair is still in Baltimore, awaiting orders. I caught the train from the Charles Street station and came back. Johnson, you know--"

"Yes, I've seen Johnson," interrupted Campbell. "Are you absolutely positive that the woman you saw get into the automobile with Mr. Cadwallader was Miss Thorne?"

"Absolutely," replied Hastings without hesitation. "I saw her in her own room with her wraps on, then saw her come down and get into the car."

"That's all," said the chief. "Good night." For an hour or more he sat in a great, comfortable chair in the smoking-room of his own home, the guileless blue eyes vacant, staring, and spidery lines in the benevolent forehead.

*   *   *   *   *

On the morning of the second day following, Senor Rodriguez, the minister from Venezuela, reported to the Secret Service Bureau the disappearance of fifty thousand dollars in gold from a safe in his private office at the legation.

IX
FIFTY THOUSAND DOLLARS

Mr. Campbell was talking.

"For several months past," he said, "the International Investment Company, through its representative, Mr. Cressy, has been secretly negotiating with Senor Rodriguez for certain asphalt properties in Venezuela. Three days ago these negotiations were successfully concluded, and yesterday afternoon Mr. Cressy, in secret, paid to Senor Rodriguez, fifty thousand dollars in American gold, the first of four payments of similar sums. This gold was to have been shipped to Philadelphia by express to-day to catch a steamer for Venezuela." Mr. Grimm nodded.

"The fact that this gold was in Senor Rodriguez's possession could not have been known to more than half a dozen persons, as the negotiations throughout have been in strict secrecy," and Mr. Campbell smiled benignly. "So much! Now, Senor Rodriguez has just telephoned asking that I send a man to the legation at once. The gold was kept there over night; or perhaps I should say that the senor intended to keep it there over night." Mr. Campbell stared at Mr. Grimm for a moment, then: "Miss Thorne, you know, is a guest at the legation, that is why I am referring the matter to you."

"I understand," said Mr. Grimm.

And ten minutes later Mr. Grimm presented himself to Senor Rodriguez. The minister from Venezuela, bubbling with excitement, was pacing forth and back across his office, ruffling his gray-black hair with nervous, twining fingers. Mr. Grimm sat down.

"Senor," he inquired placidly, "fifty thousand dollars in gold would weigh nearly two hundred pounds, wouldn't it?"

Senor Rodriguez stared at him blankly.

"Si, Senor," he agreed absently. And then, in English: "Yes, I should imagine so."

"Well, was all of it stolen, or only a part of it?" Mr. Grimm went on.

The minister gazed into the listless eyes for a time, then, apparently bewildered, walked forth and back across the room again. Finally he sat down.

"All of it," he admitted. "I can't understand it. No one, not a soul in this house, except myself, knew it was here."

"In addition to this weight of, say two hundred pounds, fifty thousand dollars would make considerable bulk," mused Mr. Grimm. "Very well! Therefore it would appear that the person, or persons, who got it must have gone away from here heavily laden?"

Senor Rodriguez nodded.

"And now, Senor," Mr. Grimm continued, "if you will kindly state the circumstances immediately preceding and following the theft?"

A slight frown which had been growing upon the smooth brow of the diplomatist was instantly dissipated.

"The money--fifty thousand dollars in gold coin--was paid to me yesterday afternoon about four o'clock," he began slowly, in explanation.

"By Mr. Cressy of the International Investment Company," supplemented Mr. Grimm. "Yes. Go on."

The diplomatist favored the young man with one sharp, inquiring glance, and continued:

"The gentleman who paid the money remained here from four until nine o'clock while I, personally, counted it. As I counted it I placed it in canvas bags and when he had gone I took these bags from this room into that," he indicated a closed door to his right, "and personally stowed them away in the safe. I closed and locked the door of the safe myself; I *know* that it *was* locked. And that's all, except this morning the money was gone--every dollar of it."

"Safe blown?" inquired Mr. Grimm.

"No, Senor!" exclaimed the diplomatist with sudden violence. "No, the safe was not blown! It was *closed and locked*, exactly as I had left it!"

Mr. Grimm was idly twisting the seal ring on his little finger.

"Just as I left it!" Senor Rodriguez repeated excitedly. "Last night after I locked the safe door I tried it to make certain that it **was** locked. I happened to notice then that the pointer on the dial had stopped precisely at number forty-five. This morning, when I unlocked the safe--and, of course, I didn't know then that the money had been taken--the pointer was still at number forty-five."

He paused with one hand in the air; Mr. Grimm continued to twist the seal ring.

"It was all like--like some trick on the stage," the minister went on, "like the magician's disappearing lady, or--or--! It was as though I had not put the money into the safe at all!"

"Did you?" inquired Mr. Grimm amiably.

"Did I?" blazed Senor Rodriguez. "Why, Senor--! I did!" he concluded meekly.

Mr. Grimm believed him.

"Who else knows the combination of the safe?" he queried.

"No one, Senor--not a living soul."

"Your secretary, for instance?"

"Not even my secretary."

"Some servant--some member of your family?"

"I tell you, Senor, not one person in all the world knew that combination except myself," Senor Rodriguez insisted.

"Your secretary--a servant--some member of your family might have seen you unlock the safe some time, and thus learned the combination?"

Senor Rodriguez did not quite know whether to be annoyed at Mr. Grimm's persistence, or to admire the tenacity with which he held to this one point.

"You must understand, Senor Grimm, that many state documents are kept in the safe," he said finally, "therefore it is not advisable that any one should know the combination. I have made it an absolute rule, as did my predecessors here, never to unlock the safe in the presence of another person."

"State documents!" Mr. Grimm's lips silently repeated the words. Then aloud: "Perhaps there's a record of the combination somewhere? If you had died suddenly, for instance, how would the safe have been opened?"

"There would have been only one way, Senor--blow it open. There is no record."

"Well, if we accept all that as true," observed Mr. Grimm musingly, "it would seem that you either didn't put the money into the safe at all, or--please sit down, there's nothing personal in this--or else the money was taken out of the safe without it being unlocked. This last would have been a miracle, and this is not the day of miracles, therefore--!"

Mr. Grimm's well modulated voice trailed off into silence. Senor Rodriguez came to his feet with a blaze of anger in his eyes; Mr. Grimm was watching him curiously.

"I understand then, Senor," said the minister deliberately, "that you believe that I--!"

"I believe that you have told the truth," interrupted Mr. Grimm placidly, "that is the truth so far as you know it. But you have stated one thing in error. Somebody besides yourself *does* know the combination. Whether they knew it or not at this time yesterday I can't say, but somebody knows it now."

Senor Rodriguez drew a deep breath of relief. The implied accusation had been withdrawn as pleasantly and frankly as it had been put forward.

"I ran across a chap in New York once, for instance," Mr. Grimm took the trouble to explain, "who could unlock any safe--that is, any safe of the kind used at that time--twelve or fourteen years ago. So you see. I doubt if he would be so successful with the new models, with all their improvements, but then--! You know he would have made an ideal burglar, that chap. Now, Senor, who lives here in the legation with you?"

"My secretary, Senor Diaz, my daughter Inez, and just at the moment, a Miss Thorne--Miss Isabel Thorne," the senor informed him. "Also four servants--two men and two women."

"I've had the pleasure of meeting your daughter and Miss Thorne," Mr. Grimm informed him. "Now, suppose we take a look at the safe?"

"Certainly."

Senor Rodriguez started toward the closed door just as there came a timid knock from the hall. He glanced at Mr. Grimm, who nodded, then he called:

"Come in!"

The door opened, and Miss Thorne entered. She was clad in some filmy, gossamer-like morning gown with her radiant hair caught up on her white neck. At sight of Mr. Grimm the blue-gray eyes opened as if in surprise, and she paused irresolutely.

"I beg your pardon, Senor," she said, addressing the diplomatist. "I did not know you were engaged. And Mr. Grimm!" She extended a slim, white hand, and the young man bowed low over it. "We are old friends," she explained, smilingly, to the minister. Then: "I think I must have dropped my handkerchief when I was in here yesterday with Inez. Perhaps you found it?"

"Si, Senorita," replied Senor Rodriguez gallantly. "It is on my desk in here. Just a moment."

He opened the door and passed into the adjoining room. Mr. Grimm's eyes met those of Miss Isabel Thorne, and there was no listlessness in them now, only interest. She smiled at him tauntingly and lowered her lids. Senor Rodriguez appeared from the other room with the handkerchief.

"Mil gracias, Senor," she thanked him.

"No hay de que, Senorita," he returned, as he opened the door for her.

"Monsieur Grimm, au revoir!" She dropped a little curtsey, and still smiling, went out.

"She is charming, Senor," the diplomatist assured him enthusiastically, albeit irrelevantly. "Such vivacity, such personality, such--such--she is charming."

"The safe, please," Mr. Grimm reminded him.

X
A SAFE OPENING

Together they entered the adjoining room, which was small compared to the one they had just left. Senor Rodriguez used it as a private office. His desk was on their right between two windows overlooking the same pleasant little garden which was visible from the suite of tiny drawing-rooms farther along. The safe, a formidable looking receptacle of black enameled steel, stood at their left, closed and locked. The remaining wall space of the room was given over to oak cabinets, evidently a storage place for the less important legation papers.

"Has any one besides yourself been in this room to-day?" Mr. Grimm inquired.

"Not a soul, Senor," was the reply.

Mr. Grimm went over and examined the windows. They were both locked inside; and there were no marks of any sort on the sills.

"They are just as I left them last night," explained Senor Rodriguez. "I have not touched them to-day."

"And there's only one door," mused Mr. Grimm, meaning that by which they had entered. "So it would appear that whoever was here last night entered through that room. Very well."

He walked around the room once, opening and shutting the doors of the cabinets as he passed, and finally paused in front of the safe. A brief examination of the nickeled dial and handle and of the enameled edges of the heavy door satisfied him that no force had been employed--the safe had merely been unlocked. Whereupon he sat himself down, cross-legged on the floor, in front of it.

"What are the first and second figures of the combination?" he asked.

"Thirty-six, then back to ten."

Mr. Grimm set the dial at thirty-six, and then, with his ear pressed closely against the polished door, turned the dial slowly back. Senor Rodriguez stood looking on helplessly, but none the less intently. The pointer read ten, then nine, eight, seven, five. Mr. Grimm gazed at it thoughtfully, after which he did it all over again, placidly and without haste.

"Now, we'll look inside, please," he requested, rising.

Senor Rodriguez unlocked the safe the while Mr. Grimm respectfully turned his eyes away, then pulled the door wide open. The books had been piled one on top of another and thrust into various pigeonholes at the top. Mr. Grimm understood that this disorder was the result of making room at the bottom for the bulk of gold, and asked no questions. Instead, he sat down upon the floor again.

"The lock on this private compartment at the top is broken," he remarked after a moment.

"Si, Senor," the diplomatist agreed. "Evidently the robbers were not content with only fifty thousand dollars in gold--they imagined that something else of value was hidden there."

"Was there?" asked Mr. Grimm naively. He didn't look around.

"Nothing of monetary value," the senor explained. "There were some important state papers in there--they are there yet--but no money."

"None of the papers was stolen?"

"No, Senor. There were only nine packets--they are there yet."

"Contents all right?"

"Yes. I personally looked them over."

Mr. Grimm drew out the packets of papers, one by one. They were all unsealed save the last. When he reached for that, Senor Rodriguez made a quick, involuntary motion toward it with his hand.

"This one's sealed," commented Mr. Grimm. "It doesn't happen that you opened it and sealed it again?"

Senor Rodriguez stood staring at him blankly for a moment, then some sudden apprehension was aroused, for a startled look came into his eyes, and again he reached for the packet.

"Dios mio!" he exclaimed, "let me see, Senor."

"Going to open it?" asked Mr. Grimm.

"Yes, Senor. I had not thought of it before."

Mr. Grimm rose and walked over to the window where the light was better. He scrutinized the sealed packet closely. There were three red splotches of wax upon it, each impressed with the legation seal; the envelope was without marks otherwise. He turned and twisted it aimlessly, and peered curiously at the various seals, after which he handed it to the frankly impatient diplomatist.

Senor Rodriguez opened it, with nervous, twitching fingers. Mr. Grimm had turned toward the safe again, but he heard the crackle of parchment as some document was drawn out of the envelope, and then came a deep sigh of relief. Having satisfied his sudden fears for the safety of the paper, whatever it was, the senor placed it in another envelope and sealed it again with elaborate care. Mr. Grimm dropped into the swivel chair at the desk.

"Senor," he inquired pleasantly, "your daughter and Miss Thorne were in this room yesterday afternoon?"

"Yes," replied the diplomatist as if surprised at the question.

"What time, please?"

"About three o'clock. They were going out driving. Why?"

"And just where, please, did you find that handkerchief?" continued Mr. Grimm.

"Handkerchief?" repeated the diplomatist. "You mean Miss Thorne's handkerchief?" He paused and regarded Mr. Grimm keenly. "Senor, what am I to understand from that question?"

"It was plain enough," replied Mr. Grimm. "Where did you find that handkerchief?" There was silence for an instant. "In this room?"

"Yes," replied Senor Rodriguez at last.

"Near the safe?" Mr. Grimm persisted.

"Yes," came the slow reply, again. "Just here," and he indicated a spot a little to the left of the safe.

"And *when* did you find it? Yesterday afternoon? Last night? This morning?"

"This morning," and without any apparent reason the diplomatist's face turned deathly white.

"But, Senor--Senor, you are mistaken! There can be nothing--! A woman! Two hundred pounds of gold! Senor!"

Mr. Grimm was still pleasant about it; his curiosity was absolutely impersonal; his eyes, grown listless again, were turned straight into the other's face.

"If that handkerchief had been there last night, Senor," he resumed quietly, "wouldn't you have noticed it when you placed the gold in the safe?"

Senor Rodriguez stared at him a long time.

"I don't know," he said, at last. He dropped back into a chair with his face in his hands. "Senor," he burst out suddenly, impetuously, after a moment, "if the gold is not recovered I am ruined. You understand that better than I can tell you. It's the kind of thing that could not be explained to my government." He rose suddenly and faced the impassive young man, with merciless determination in his face. "You must find the gold, Senor," he said.

"No matter who may be--who may suffer?" inquired Mr. Grimm.

"Find the gold, Senor!"

"Very well," commented Mr. Grimm, without moving. "Do me the favor, please, to regain possession of the handkerchief you just returned to Miss Thorne, and to send to me here your secretary, Senor Diaz, and your servants, one by one. I shall question them alone. No, don't be alarmed. Unless they know of the robbery they shall get no inkling of it from me. First, be good enough to replace the packet in the safe, and lock it."

Senor Rodriguez replaced the packet without question, afterward locking the door, then went out. A moment later Senor Diaz appeared. He remained with Mr. Grimm for just eight minutes. Senor Rodriguez entered again as his secretary passed on, and laid a lace handkerchief on the desk. Mr. Grimm stared at it curiously for a long time.

"It's the same handkerchief?"

"Si, Senor."

"There's no doubt whatever about it?"

"No, Senor, I got it by--!"

"It's of no consequence," interrupted Mr. Grimm. "Now the servants, please-- the men first."

The first of the men servants was in the room two minutes; the second--the butler--was there five minutes; one of the women was not questioned at all; the other remained ten minutes. Mr. Grimm followed her into the hall; Senor Rodriguez stood there helpless, impatient.

"Well?" he demanded eagerly.

"I'm going out a little while," replied Mr. Grimm placidly. "No one has even an intimation of the affair--please keep the matter absolutely to yourself until I return."

That was all. The door opened and closed, and he was gone.

At the end of an hour he returned, passed on through to the diplomatist's private office, sat down in front of the locked safe again, and set the dial at thirty-six. Senor Rodriguez looked on, astonished, as Mr. Grimm pressed the soft rubber sounder of a stethoscope against the safe door and began turning the dial back toward ten, slowly, slowly. Thirty-five minutes later the lock clicked. Mr. Grimm rose, turned the handle, and pulled the safe door open.

"That's how it was done," he explained to the amazed diplomatist. "And now, please, have a servant hand my card to Miss Thorne."

XI
THE LACE HANDKERCHIEF

Still wearing the graceful, filmy morning gown, with an added touch, of scarlet in her hair--a single red rose--Miss Thorne came into the drawing-room where Mr. Grimm sat waiting. There was curiosity in her manner, thinly veiled, but the haunting smile still lingered about her lips. Mr. Grimm bowed low, and placed a chair for her, after which he stood for a time staring down at one slim, white hand at rest on the arm of the seat. At last, he, too, sat down.

"I believe," he said slowly, without preliminaries, "this is your handkerchief?"

He offered the lacy trifle, odd in design, unique in workmanship, obviously of foreign texture, and she accepted it.

"Yes," she agreed readily, "I must have dropped it again."

"That is the one handed to you by Senor Rodriguez," Mr. Grimm told her. "I think you said you lost it in his office yesterday afternoon?"

"Yes?" She nodded inquiringly.

"It may interest you to know that Senor Rodriguez's butler positively identifies it as one he restored to you twice at dinner last evening, between seven and nine o'clock," Mr. Grimm went on dispassionately.

"Indeed!" exclaimed Miss Thorne.

"The senor identifies it as one he found this morning in his office," Mr. Grimm explained obligingly. "During the night fifty thousand dollars in gold were stolen from his safe."

There was not the slightest change of expression in her face; the blue-gray eyes were still inquiring in their gaze, the white hands still at rest, the scarlet lips still curled slightly, an echo of a smile.

"No force was used in opening the safe," Mr. Grimm resumed. "It was unlocked. It's an old model and I have demonstrated how it could have been opened either with the assistance of a stethoscope, which catches the sound of the tumbler in the lock, or by a person of acute hearing."

Miss Thorne sat motionless, waiting.

"All this means--what?" she inquired, at length.

"I'll trouble you, please, to return the money," requested Mr. Grimm courteously. "No reason appears why you should have taken it. But I'm not seeking reasons, nor am I seeking disagreeable publicity--only the money."

"It seems to me you attach undue importance to the handkerchief," she objected.

"That's a matter of opinion," Mr. Grimm remarked. "It would be useless, even tedious, to attempt to disprove a burglar theory, but against it is the difficulty of entrance, the weight of the gold, the ingenious method of opening the safe, and the assumption that not more than six persons knew the money was in the safe; while a person in the house *might* have learned it in any of a dozen ways. And, in addition, is the fact that the handkerchief is odd, therefore noticeable. A lace expert assures me there's probably not another like it in the world."

He stopped. Miss Thorne's eyes sparkled and a smile seemed to be tugging at the corners of her mouth. She spread out the handkerchief on her knees.

"You could identify this again, of course?" she queried.

"Yes."

She thoughtfully crumpled up the bit of lace in both hands, then opened them. There were two handkerchiefs now--they were identical.

"Which is it, please?" she asked.

If Mr. Grimm was disappointed there was not a trace of it on his face. She laughed outright, gleefully, mockingly, then, demurely:

"Pardon me! You see, it's absurd. The handkerchief the butler restored to me at dinner, after I lost one in the senor's office, might have been either of these, or one of ten other duplicates in my room, all given to me by her Maj--I mean," she corrected quickly, "by a friend in Europe." She was silent for a moment. "Is that all?"

"No," replied Mr. Grimm gravely, decisively. "I'm not satisfied. I shall insist upon the return of the money, and if it is not forthcoming I dare say Count di Rosini, the Italian ambassador, would be pleased to give his personal check rather than have the matter become public." She started to interrupt; he went on. "In any event you will be requested to leave the country."

Then, and not until then, a decided change came over Miss Thorne's face. A deeper color leaped to her cheeks, the smile faded from her lips, and there was a flash of uneasiness in her eyes.

"But if I am innocent?" she protested.

"You must prove it," continued Mr. Grimm mercilessly. "Personally, I am convinced, and Count di Rosini has practically assured me that--"

"It's unjust!" she interrupted passionately. "It's--it's--you have proved nothing. It's unheard of! It's beyond--!"

Suddenly she became silent. A minute, two minutes, three minutes passed; Mr. Grimm waited patiently.

"Will you give me time and opportunity to prove my innocence?" she demanded finally. "And if I *do* convince you--?"

"I should be delighted to believe that I have made a mistake," Mr. Grimm assured her. "How much time? One day? Two days?"

"I will let you know within an hour at your office," she told him.

Mr. Grimm rose.

"And meanwhile, in case of accident, I shall look to Count di Rosini for adjustment," he added pointedly. "Good morning."

One hour and ten minutes later he received this note, unsigned:

"Closed carriage will stop for you at southeast corner of Pennsylvania Avenue and Fourteenth Street to-night at one."

He was there; the carriage was on time; and my lady of mystery was inside. He stepped in and they swung out into Pennsylvania Avenue, noiselessly over the asphalt.

"Should the gold be placed in your hands now, within the hour," she queried solicitously, "would it be necessary for you to know who was the--the thief?"

"It would," Mr. Grimm responded without hesitation.

"Even if it destroyed a reputation?" she pleaded.

"The Secret Service rarely destroys a reputation, Miss Thorne, although it holds itself in readiness to do so. I dare say in this case there would be no arrest or prosecution, because of--of reasons which appear to be good."

"There wouldn't?" and there was a note of eagerness in her voice. "The identity of the guilty person would never appear?"

"It would become a matter of record in our office, but beyond that I think not--at least in this one instance."

Miss Thorne sat silent for a block or more.

"You'll admit, Mr. Grimm, that you have forced me into a most remarkable position. You seemed convinced of my guilt, and, if you'll pardon me, without reason; then you made it compulsory upon me to establish my innocence. The only way for me to do that was to find the guilty one. I have done it, and I'm sorry, because it's a little tragedy."

Mr. Grimm waited.

"It's a girl high in diplomatic society. Her father's position is an honorable rather than a lucrative one; he has no fortune. This girl moves in a certain set devoted to bridge, and stakes are high. She played and won, and played and won, and on and on, until her winnings were about eight thousand dollars. Then luck turned. She began to lose. Her money went, but she continued to play desperately. Finally some old family jewels were pawned without her father's knowledge, and ultimately they were lost. One day she awoke to the fact that she owed some nine or ten thousand dollars in bridge debts. They were pressing and there was no way to meet them. This meant exposure and utter ruin, and women do strange things, Mr. Grimm, to postpone such an ending to social aspirations. I know this much is true, for she related it all to me herself.

"At last, in some way--a misplaced letter, perhaps, or a word overheard--she learned that fifty thousand dollars would be in the legation safe overnight, and evidently she learned the precise night." She paused a moment. "Here is the address of a man in Baltimore, Thomas Q. Griswold," and she passed a card to Mr. Grimm, who sat motionless, listening. "About four years ago the combination on the legation safe was changed. This man was sent here to make the change, therefore some one besides Senor Rodriguez *does* know the combination. I have communicated with this man to-day, for I saw the possibility of just such a thing as this instead of your stethoscope. By a trick and a forged letter this girl obtained the combination from this man."

Mr. Grimm drew a long breath.

"She intended to take, perhaps, only what she desperately needed--but at sight of it all--do you see what must have been the temptation then? We get out here."

There were many unanswered questions in Mr. Grimm's mind. He repressed them for the time, stepped out and assisted Miss Thorne to alight. The carriage had turned out of Pennsylvania Avenue, and at the moment he didn't quite place himself. A narrow passageway opened before them--evidently the rear entrance to a house possibly in the next street. Miss Thorne led the way unhesitatingly, cautiously unlocked the door, and together they entered a hall. Then there was a short flight of stairs, and they stepped into a room, one of a suite. She closed the door and turned on the lights.

"The bags of gold are in the next room," she said with the utmost composure.

Mr. Grimm dragged them out of a dark closet, opened one--there were ten-- and allowed the coins to dribble through his fingers. Finally he turned and stared at Miss Thorne, who, pallid and weary, stood looking on.

"Where are we?" he asked. "What house is this?"

"The Venezuelan legation," she answered. "We are standing less than forty feet from the safe that was robbed. You see how easy--!"

"And whose room?" inquired Mr. Grimm slowly.

"Must I answer?" she asked appealingly.

"You must!"

"Senorita Rodriguez--my hostess! Don't you see what you've made me do? She and Mr. Cadwallader made the trip to Baltimore in his automobile, and--and--!" She stopped. "He knows nothing of it," she added.

"Yes, I know," said Mr. Grimm.

He stood looking at her in silence for a moment, staring deeply into the pleading eyes; and a certain tense expression about his lips passed. For an instant her hand trembled on his arm, and he caught the fragrance of her hair.

"Where is she now?" he asked.

"Playing bridge," replied Miss Thorne, with a sad little smile. "It is always so-- at least twice a week, and she rarely returns before two or half-past." She extended both hands impetuously, entreatingly. "Please be generous, Mr. Grimm. You have the gold; don't destroy her."

Senor Rodriguez, the minister from Venezuela, found the gold in his safe on the following morning, with a brief note from Mr. Grimm, in which there was no explanation of how or where it had been found.... And two hours later Monsieur Boissegur, ambassador from France to the United States, disappeared from the embassy, vanished!

XII
THE VANISHING DIPLOMATIST

It was three days after the ambassador's disappearance that Monsieur Rigolot, secretary of the French embassy and temporary *charge-d'affaires*, reported the matter to Chief Campbell in the Secret Service Bureau, adding thereto a detailed statement of several singular incidents following close upon it. He told it in order, concisely and to the point, while Grimm and his chief listened.

"Monsieur Boissegur, the ambassador, you understand, is a man whose habits are remarkably regular," he began. "He has made it a rule to be at his desk every morning at ten o'clock, and between that time and one o'clock he dictates his correspondence, and clears up whatever routine work there is before him. I have known him for many years, and have been secretary of the embassy under him in Germany and Japan and this country. I have never known him to vary this general order of work unless because of illness, or necessary absence.

"Well, Monsieur, last Tuesday--this is Friday--the ambassador was at his desk as usual. He dictated a dozen or more letters, and had begun another--a private letter to his sister in Paris. He was well along in this letter when, without any apparent reason, he rose from his desk and left the room, closing the door behind him. His stenographer's impression was that some detail of business had occurred to him, and he had gone into the general office farther down the hall to attend to it. I may say, Monsieur, that this impression seemed strengthened by the fact that he left a fresh cigarette burning in his ash tray, and his pen was behind his ear. It was all as if he had merely stepped out, intending to return immediately--the sort of thing, Monsieur, that any man might have done.

"It so happened that when he went out he left a sentence of his letter incomplete. I tell you this to show that the impulse to go must have been a sudden one, yet there was nothing in his manner, so his stenographer says, to indicate excitement, or any other than his usual frame of mind. It was about five minutes of twelve o'clock--high noon--when he went out. When he didn't return immediately the stenographer began transcribing the letters. At one o'clock Monsieur Boissegur still had not returned and his stenographer went to luncheon."

As he talked some inbred excitement seemed to be growing upon him, due, perhaps, to his recital of the facts, and he paused at last to regain control of himself. Incidentally he wondered if Mr. Grimm was taking the slightest interest in what he was saying. Certainly there was nothing in his impassive face to indicate it.

"Understand, Monsieur," the secretary continued, after a moment, "that I knew nothing whatever of all this until late that afternoon--that is, Tuesday afternoon about five o'clock. I was engaged all day upon some important work in my own office, and had had no occasion to see Monsieur Boissegur since a word or so when he came in at ten o'clock. My attention was called to the affair finally by his stenographer, Monsieur Netterville, who came to me for instructions. He had finished the letters and the ambassador had not returned to sign them. At this point I began an investigation, Monsieur, and the further I went the more uneasy I grew.

"Now, Monsieur, there are only two entrances to the embassy--the front door, where a servant is in constant attendance from nine in the morning until ten at night, and the rear door, which can only be reached through the kitchen. Neither of the two men who had been stationed at the front door had seen the ambassador since breakfast, therefore he could not have gone out that way. *Comprenez*? It seemed ridiculous, Monsieur, but then I went to the kitchen. The *chef* had been there all day, and he had not seen the ambassador at all. I inquired further. No one in the embassy, not a clerk, nor a servant, nor a member of the ambassador's family had seen him since he left his office."

Again he paused and ran one hand across his troubled brow.

"Monsieur," he went on, and there was a tense note in his voice, "the ambassador of France had disappeared, gone, vanished! We searched the house from the cellar to the servants' quarters, even the roof, but there was no trace of him. The hat he usually wore was in the hall, and all his other hats were accounted for. You may remember, Monsieur, that Tuesday was cold, but all his top-coats were found in their proper places. So it seems, Monsieur," and repression ended in a burst of excitement, "if he left the embassy he did not go out by either door, and he went without hat or coat!"

He stopped helplessly and his gaze alternated inquiringly between the benevolent face of the chief and the expressionless countenance of Mr. Grimm.

"If he left the embassy?" Mr. Grimm repeated. "If your search of the house proved conclusively that he wasn't there, he *did* leave it, didn't he?"

Monsieur Rigolot stared at him blankly for a moment, then nodded.

"And there are windows, you know," Mr. Grimm went on, then: "As I understand it, Monsieur, no one except you and the stenographer saw the ambassador after ten o'clock in the morning?"

"Oui, Monsieur. C'est--" Monsieur Rigolot began excitedly. "I beg pardon. I believe that is correct."

"You saw him about ten, you say; therefore no one except the stenographer saw him after ten o'clock?"

"That is also true, as far as I know."

"Any callers? Letters? Telegrams? Telephone messages?"

"I made inquiries in that direction, Monsieur," was the reply. "I have the words of the servants at the door and of the stenographer that there were no callers, and the statement of the stenographer that there were no telephone calls or telegrams. There were only four letters for him personally. He left them all on his desk--here they are."

Mr. Grimm looked them over leisurely. They were commonplace enough, containing nothing that might be construed into a reason for the disappearance.

"The letters Monsieur Boissegur had dictated were laid on his desk by the stenographer," Monsieur Rigolot rushed on volubly, excitedly. "In the anxiety and uneasiness following the disappearance they were allowed to remain there overnight. On Wednesday morning, Monsieur"--and he hesitated impressively--"those letters bore his signature in his own handwriting!"

Mr. Grimm turned his listless eyes full upon Monsieur Rigolot's perturbed face for one scant instant.

"No doubt of it being his signature?" he queried.

"Non, Monsieur, non!" the secretary exclaimed emphatically. "Vous avez--that is, I have known his signature for years. There is no doubt. The letters were not of a private nature. If you would care to look at copies of them?"

He offered the duplicates tentatively. Mr. Grimm read them over slowly, the while Monsieur Rigolot sat nervously staring at him. They, too, seemed meaningless as bearing on the matter in hand. Finally, Mr. Grimm nodded, and Monsieur Rigolot resumed:

"And Wednesday night, Monsieur, another strange thing happened. Monsieur Boissegur smokes many cigarettes, of a kind made especially for him in France, and shipped to him here. He keeps them in a case on his dressing-table. On Thursday morning his valet reported to me that *this case of cigarettes had disappeared*!"

"Of course," observed Mr. Grimm, "Monsieur Boissegur has a latch-key to the embassy?"

"Of course."

"Anything unusual happen last night--that is, Thursday night?"

"Nothing, Monsieur--that is, nothing we can find."

Mr. Grimm was silent for a time and fell to twisting the seal ring on his finger. Mr. Campbell turned around and moved a paper weight one inch to the left, where it belonged, while Monsieur Rigolot, disappointed at their amazing apathy, squirmed uneasily in his chair.

"It would appear, then," Mr. Grimm remarked musingly, "that after his mysterious disappearance the ambassador has either twice returned to his house at night, or else sent some one there, first to bring the letters to him for signature, and later to get his cigarettes?"

"Certainement, Monsieur--I mean, that seems to be true. But where is he? Why should he not come back? What does it mean? Madame Boissegur is frantic, prostrated! She wanted me to go to the police, but I did not think it wise that it should become public, so I came here."

"Very well," commented Mr. Grimm. "Let it rest as it is. Meanwhile you may reassure madame. Point out to her that if Monsieur Boissegur signed the letters Tuesday night he was, at least, alive; and if he came or sent for the cigarettes Wednesday night, he was still alive. I shall call at the embassy this afternoon. No, it isn't advisable to go with you now. Give me your latch-key, please."

Monsieur Rigolot produced the key and passed it over without a word.

"And one other thing," Mr. Grimm continued, "please collect all the revolvers that may be in the house and take charge of them yourself. If any one, by chance, heard a burglar prowling around there to-night he might shoot, and in that event either kill Monsieur Boissegur or--or me!"

When the secretary had gone Mr. Campbell idly drummed on his desk as he studied the face of his subordinate.

"So much!" he commented finally.

"It's Miss Thorne again," said the young man as if answering a question.

"Perhaps these reports I have received to-day from the Latin capitals may aid you in dispelling that mystery," Campbell suggested, and Mr. Grimm turned to them eagerly. "Meanwhile our royal visitor, Prince Benedetto d'Abruzzi, remains unknown?"

The young man's teeth closed with a snap.

"It's only a question of time, Chief," he said abruptly. "I'll find him--I'll find him!"

And he sat down to read the reports.

XIII
A CONFERENCE IN THE DARK

The white rays of a distant arc light filtered through the half-drawn velvet hangings and laid a faintly illumined path across the ambassador's desk; the heavy leather chairs were mere impalpable splotches in the shadows; the cut-glass knobs of a mahogany cabinet caught the glint of light and reflected it dimly. Outside was the vague, indefinable night drone of a city asleep, unbroken by any sound that was distinguishable, until finally there came the distant boom of a clock. It struck twice.

Seated on a couch in one corner of the ambassador's office was Mr. Grimm. He was leaning against the high arm of leather, with his feet on the seat, thoughtfully nursing his knees. If his attitude indicated anything except sheer comfort, it was that he was listening. He had been there for two hours, wide-awake, and absolutely motionless. Five, ten, fifteen minutes more passed, and then Mr. Grimm heard the grind and whir of an automobile a block or so away, coming toward the embassy. Now it was in front.

"Honk! Hon-on-onk!" it called plaintively. "Hon-on-onk! Honk!"

The signal! At last! The automobile went rushing on, full tilt, while Mr. Grimm removed his feet from the seat and dropped them noiselessly to the floor. Thus, with his hands on his knees, and listening, listening with every faculty strained, he sat motionless, peering toward the open door that led into the hall. The car was gone now, the sound of it was swallowed up in the distance, still he sat there. It was obviously some noise in the house for which he was waiting.

Minute after minute passed, and still nothing. There was not even the whisper of a wind-stirred drapery. He was about to rise when, suddenly, with no other noise than that of the sharp click of the switch, the electric lights in the room blazed up brilliantly. The glare dazzled Mr. Grimm with its blinding flood, but he didn't move. Then softly, almost in a whisper:

"Good evening, Mr. Grimm."

It was a woman's voice, pleasant, unsurprised, perfectly modulated. Mr. Grimm certainly did not expect it now, but he knew it instantly--there was not another quite like it in the wide, wide world--and though he was still blinking a little, he came to his feet courteously.

"Good morning, Miss Thorne," he corrected gravely.

Now his vision was clearing, and he saw her, a graceful figure, silhouetted against the rich green of the wall draperies. Her lips were curled the least bit, as if she might have been smiling, and her wonderful eyes reflected a glint of--of--was it amusement? The folds of her evening dress fell away from her, and one bare, white arm was extended, as her hand still rested on the switch.

"And you didn't hear me?" still in the half whisper. "I didn't think you would. Now I'm going to put out the lights for an instant, while you pull the shades down, and then--then we must have a--a conference."

The switch snapped. The lights died as suddenly as they had been born, and Mr. Grimm, moving noiselessly, visited each of the four windows in turn. Then the lights blazed brilliantly again.

"Just for a moment," Miss Thorne explained to him quietly, and she handed him a sheet of paper. "I want you to read this--read it carefully--then I shall turn out the lights again. They are dangerous. After that we may discuss the matter at our leisure."

Mr. Grimm read the paper while Miss Thorne's eyes questioned his impassive face. At length he looked up indolently, listlessly, and the switch snapped. She crossed the room and sat down; Mr. Grimm sat beside her.

"I think," Miss Thorne suggested tentatively, "that that accounts perfectly for Monsieur Boissegur's disappearance."

"It gives one explanation, at least," Mr. Grimm assented musingly. "Kidnapped--held prisoner--fifty thousand dollars demanded for his safety and release." A pause. "And to whom, may I ask, was this demand addressed?"

"To Madame Boissegur," replied Miss Thorne. "I have the envelope in which it came. It was mailed at the general post-office at half-past one o'clock this afternoon, so the canceling stamp shows, and the envelope was addressed, as the letter was written, on a typewriter."

"And how," inquired Mr. Grimm, after a long pause, "how did it come into your possession?" He waited a little. "Why didn't Monsieur Rigolot report this development to me this afternoon when I was here?"

"Monsieur Rigolot did not inform you of it because he didn't know of it himself," she replied, answering the last question first. "It came into my possession directly from the hands of Madame Boissegur--she gave it to me."

"Why?"

Mr. Grimm was peering through the inscrutable darkness, straight into her face--a white daub in the gloom, shapeless, indistinct.

"I have known Madame Boissegur for half a dozen years," Miss Thorne continued, in explanation. "We have been friends that long. I met her first in Tokio, later in Berlin, and within a few weeks, here in Washington. You see I have traveled in the time I have been an agent for my government. Well, Madame Boissegur received this letter about half-past four o'clock this afternoon; and about half-past five she sent for me and placed it in my hands, together with all the singular details following upon the ambassador's disappearance. So, it would seem that you and I are allies for this once, and the problem is already solved. There merely remains the task of finding and releasing the ambassador."

Mr. Grimm sat perfectly still.

"And why," he asked slowly, "are you here now?"

"For the same reason that you are here," she replied readily, "to see for myself if the--the person who twice came here at night--once for the ambassador's letters and once for his cigarettes--would, by any chance, make another trip. I knew you were here, of course."

"You knew I was here," repeated Mr. Grimm musingly. "And, may I--?"

"Just as you knew that I, or some one, at least, had entered this house a few minutes ago," she interrupted. "The automobile horn outside was a signal, wasn't it? Hastings was in the car? Or was it Blair or Johnson?"

Mr. Grimm did not say.

"Didn't you anticipate any personal danger when you entered?" he queried instead. "Weren't you afraid I might shoot?"

"No."

There was a long silence. Mr. Grimm still sat with his elbows on his knees, staring, staring at the vague white splotch which was Miss Thorne's face and bare neck. One of her white arms hung at her side like a pallid serpent, and her hand was at rest on the seat of the couch.

"It seems, Miss Thorne," he said at length, casually, quite casually, "that our paths of duty are inextricably tangled. Twice previously we have met under circumstances that were more than strange, and now--this! Whatever injustice I may have done you in the past by my suspicions has, I hope, been forgiven; and in each instance we were able to work side by side toward a conclusion. I am wondering now if this singular affair will take a similar course."

He paused. Miss Thorne started to speak, but he silenced her with a slight gesture of his hand.

"It is only fair to you to say that we--that is, the Secret Service--have learned many things about you," he resumed in the same casual tone. "We have, through our foreign agents, traced you step by step from Rome to Washington. We know that you are, in a way, a representative of a sovereign of Europe; we know that you were on a secret mission to the Spanish court, perhaps for this sovereign, and remained in Madrid for a month; we know that from there you went to Paris, also on a secret mission--perhaps the same--and remained there for three weeks; we know that you met diplomatic agents of those governments later in London. We know all this; we know the manner of your coming to this country; of your coming to Washington. But we don't know *why* you are here."

Again she started to speak, and again he stopped her.

"We don't know your name, but that is of no consequence. We *do* know that in Spain you were Senora Cassavant, in Paris Mademoiselle d'Aubinon, in London Miss Jane Kellog, and here Miss Isabel Thorne. We realize that exigencies arise in your calling, and mine, which make changes of name desirable, necessary even, and there is no criticism of that. Now as the representative of your government-- rather *a* government--you have a right to be here, although unaccredited; you have a right to remain here as long as your acts are consistent with our laws; you have a right to your secrets as long as they do not, directly or indirectly, threaten the welfare of this country. Now, why are you here?"

He received no answer; he expected none. After a moment he went on:

"Admitting that you are a secret agent of Italy, admitting everything that you claim to be, you haven't convinced me that you are not the person who came here for the letters and cigarettes. You have said nothing to prove to my satisfaction that you are not the individual I was waiting for to-night."

"You don't mean that you suspect--?" she began in a tone of amazement.

"I don't mean that I suspect anything," he interposed. "I mean merely that you haven't convinced me. There's nothing inconsistent in the fact that you are what you say you are, and that in spite of that, you came to-night for--"

He was interrupted by a laugh, a throaty, silvery note that he remembered well. His idle hands closed spasmodically, only to be instantly relaxed.

"Suppose, Mr. Grimm, I should tell you that immediately after Madame Bois-segur placed the matter in my hands this afternoon I went straight to your office to show this letter to you and to ask your assistance?" she inquired. "Suppose that I left my card for you with a clerk there on being informed that you were out--remember I knew you were on the case from Madame Boissegur--would that indicate anything except that I wanted to put the matter squarely before you, and work with you?"

"We will suppose that much," Mr. Grimm agreed.

"That is a statement of fact," Miss Thorne added. "My card, which you will find at your office, will show that. And when I left your office I went to the hotel where you live, with the same purpose. You were not there, and I left a card for you. And *that* is a statement of fact. It was not difficult, owing to the extraordinary circumstances, to imagine that you would be here to-night--just as you are--and I came here. My purpose, still, was to inform you of what I knew, and work with you. Does that convince you?"

"And how did you enter the embassy?" Mr. Grimm persisted.

"Not with a latch-key, as you did," she replied. "Madame Boissegur, at my suggestion, left the French window in the hall there unfastened, and I came in that way--the way, I may add, that *Monsieur l'Ambassadeur* went out when he disappeared."

"Very well!" commented Mr. Grimm, and finally: "I think, perhaps, I owe you an apology, Miss Thorne--another one. The circumstances now, as they were at our previous meetings, are so unusual that--is it necessary to go on?" There was a certain growing deference in his tone. "I wonder if you account for Monsieur Bois-segur's disappearance as I do?" he inquired.

"I dare say," and Miss Thorne leaned toward him with sudden eagerness in her manner and voice. "Your theory is--?" she questioned.

"If we believe the servants we know that Monsieur Boissegur did not go out either by the front door or rear," Mr. Grimm explained. "That being true the French window by which you entered seems to have been the way."

"Yes, yes," Miss Thorne interpolated. "And the circumstances attending the disappearance? How do you account for the fact that he went, evidently of his own will?"

"Precisely as you must account for it if you have studied the situation here as I have," responded Mr. Grimm. "For instance, sitting at his desk there"--and he turned to indicate it--"he could readily see out the windows overlooking the street. There is only a narrow strip of lawn between the house and the sidewalk. Now, if some one on the sidewalk, or--or--"

"In a carriage?" promptly suggested Miss Thorne.

"Or in a carriage," Mr. Grimm supplemented, "had attracted his attention--some one he knew--it is not at all unlikely that he rose, for no apparent reason, as he did do, passed along the hall--"

"And through the French window, across the lawn to the carriage, and not a person in the house would have seen him go out? Precisely! There seems no doubt that was the way," she mused. "And, of course, he must have entered the carriage of his own free will?"

"In other words, on some pretext or other, he was lured in, then made prisoner, and--!"

He paused suddenly and his hand met Miss Thorne's warningly. The silence of the night was broken by the violent clatter of footsteps, apparently approaching the embassy. The noise was unmistakable--some one was running.

"The window!" Miss Thorne whispered.

She rose quickly and started to cross the room, to look out; Mr. Grimm sat motionless, listening. An instant later and there came a tremendous crash of glass--the French window in the hallway by the sound--then rapid footsteps, still running, along the hall. Mr. Grimm moved toward the door unruffled, perfectly self-possessed; there was only a narrowing of his eyes at the abruptness and clatter of it all. And then the electric lights in the hall flashed up.

Before Mr. Grimm stood a man, framed by the doorway, staring unseeingly into the darkened room. His face was haggard and white as death; his mouth agape as if from exertion, and the lips bloodless; his eyes were widely distended as if from fright--clothing disarranged, collar unfastened and dangling.

"The ambassador!" Miss Thorne whispered thrillingly.

XIV
A RESCUE AND AN ESCAPE

Miss Thorne's voice startled Mr. Grimm a little, but he had no doubts. It was Monsieur Boissegur. Mr. Grimm was going toward the enframed figure when, without any apparent reason, the ambassador turned and ran along the hall; and at that instant the lights went out again. For one moment Grimm stood still, dazed and blinded by the sudden blackness, and again he started toward the door. Miss Thorne was beside him.

"The lights!" he whispered tensely. "Find the switch!"

He heard the rustle of her skirts as she moved away, and stepped out into the hall, feeling with both his hands along the wall. A few feet away, in the direction the ambassador had gone, there seemed to be a violent struggle in progress--there was the scuffling of feet, and quick-drawn breaths as muscle strained against muscle. The lights! If he could only find the switch! Then, as his hands moved along the wall, they came in contact with another hand--a hand pressed firmly against the plastering, barring his progress. A light blow in the face caused him to step back quickly.

The scuffling sound suddenly resolved itself into moving footsteps, and the front door opened and closed with a bang. Mr. Grimm's listless eyes snapped, and his white teeth came together sharply as he started toward the front door. But fate seemed to be against him still. He stumbled over a chair, and his own impetus forward sent him sprawling; his head struck the wall with a resounding whack; and then, over the house, came utter silence. From outside he heard the clatter of a cab. Finally that died away in the distance.

"Miss Thorne?" he inquired quietly.

"I'm here," she answered in a despairing voice. "But I can't find the switch."

"Are you hurt?"

"No."

And then she found the switch; the lights flared up. Mr. Grimm was sitting thoughtfully on the floor.

"That simplifies the matter considerably," he observed complacently, as he rose. "The men who signaled to me when you entered the embassy will never let that cab get out of their sight."

Miss Thorne stood leaning forward a little, eagerly gazing at him with those wonderful blue-gray eyes, and an expression of--of--perhaps it was admiration on her face.

"Are you sure?" she demanded, at last.

"I know it," was his response.

And just then Monsieur Rigolot, secretary of the embassy, thrust an inquisitive head timidly around the corner of the stairs. The crash of glass had aroused him.

"What happened?" he asked breathlessly.

"We don't know just yet," replied Mr. Grimm. "If the noise aroused any one else please assure them that there's nothing the matter. And you might inform Madame Boissegur that the ambassador will return home to-morrow. Good night!"

At his hotel, when he reached there, Mr. Grimm found Miss Thorne's card--and he drew a long breath; at his office he found another of her cards, and he drew another long breath. He did like corroborative details, did Mr. Grimm, and, of course, this--! On the following day Miss Thorne accompanied him to Alexandria, and they were driven in a closed carriage out toward the western edge of the city. Finally the carriage stopped at a signal from Mr. Grimm, and he assisted Miss Thorne out, after which he turned and spoke to some one remaining inside--a man.

"The house is two blocks west, along that street there," he explained, and he indicated an intersecting thoroughfare just ahead. "It is number ninety-seven. Five minutes after we enter you will drive up in front of the door and wait. If we don't return in fifteen minutes--come in after us!"

"Do you anticipate danger?" Miss Thorne queried quickly.

"If I had anticipated danger," replied Mr. Grimm, "I should not have permitted you to come with me."

They entered the house--number ninety-seven--with a key which Mr. Grimm produced, and a minute or so later walked into a room where three men were sitting. One of them was of a coarse, repulsive type, large and heavy; another rather dapper, of superficial polish, evidently a foreigner, and the third--the third was Ambassador Boissegur!

"Good morning, gentlemen!" Mr. Grimm greeted them, then ceremoniously: "Monsieur Boissegur, your carriage is at the door."

The three men came to their feet instantly, and one of them--he of the heavy face--drew a revolver. Mr. Grimm faced him placidly.

"Do you know what would happen to you if you killed me?" he inquired pleasantly. "You wouldn't live three minutes. Do you imagine I came in here blindly? There are a dozen men guarding the entrances to the house--a pistol shot would bring them in. Put down the gun!"

Eyes challenged eyes for one long tense instant, and the man carefully laid the weapon on the table. Mr. Grimm strolled over and picked it up, after which he glanced inquiringly at the other man--the ambassador's second guard.

"And you are the gentleman, I dare say, who made the necessary trips to the ambassador's house, probably using his latch-key?" he remarked interrogatively. "First for the letters to be signed, and again for the cigarettes?"

There was no answer and Mr. Grimm turned questioningly to Monsieur Boissegur, silent, white of face, motionless.

"Yes, Monsieur," the ambassador burst out suddenly. His eyes were fixed unwaveringly on Miss Thorne.

"And your escape, Monsieur?" continued Mr. Grimm.

"I did escape, Monsieur, last night," the ambassador explained, "but they knew it immediately--they pursued me into my own house, these two and another--and dragged me back here! *Mon Dieu, Monsieur, c'est--!*"

"That's all that's necessary," remarked Mr. Grimm. "You are free to go now."

"But there are others," Monsieur Boissegur interposed desperately, "two more somewhere below, and they will not allow--they will attack--!"

Mr. Grimm's listless eyes narrowed slightly and he turned to Miss Thorne. She was a little white, but he saw enough in her face to satisfy him.

"I shall escort Monsieur Boissegur to his carriage, Miss Thorne," he said calmly. "These men will remain here until I return. Take the revolver. If either of them so much as wags his head--shoot! You are not--not afraid?"

"No." She smiled faintly. "I am not afraid."

Mr. Grimm and the ambassador went down the stairs, and out the front door. Mr. Grimm was just turning to reenter the house when from above came a muffled, venomous cra-as-ash!--a shot! He took the steps going up, two at a time. Miss Thorne was leaning against the wall as if dazed; the revolver lay at her feet. A door in a far corner of the room stood open; and the clatter of footsteps echoed through the house.

"One of them leaped at me and I fired," she gasped in explanation. "He struck me, but I'm--I'm not hurt."

She stooped quickly, picked up the revolver and made as if to follow the dying footsteps. Mr. Grimm stopped her.

"It doesn't matter," he said quietly. "Let them go." And after a while, earnestly: "If I had dreamed of such a--such a thing as this I should never have consented to allow you--"

"I understand," she interrupted, and for one instant her outstretched hand rested on his arm. "The ambassador?"

"Perfectly safe," responded Mr. Grimm. "Two of my men are with him."

XV
MASTER OF THE SITUATION

As the women rose and started out, leaving the gentlemen over their coffee and cigars, Miss Thorne paused at the door and the blue-gray eyes flashed some subtle message to the French ambassador who, after an instant, nodded comprehendingly, then resumed his conversation. As he left the room a few minutes later he noticed that Mr. Grimm had joined a group of automaniacs of which Mr. Cadwallader was the enthusiastic center. He spoke to his hostess, the wife of the minister from Portugal, for a moment, then went to Miss Thorne and dropped into a seat beside her. She greeted him with a smile and was still smiling as she talked.

"I believe, Monsieur," she said in French, "you sent a code message to the cable office this afternoon?"

His eyes questioned hers quickly.

"And please bear in mind that we probably are being watched as we talk," she went on pleasantly. "Mr. Grimm is the man to be afraid of. Smile--don't look so serious!" She laughed outright.

"Yes, I sent a code message," he replied.

"It was your resignation?"

"Yes."

"Well, it wasn't sent, of course," she informed him, and her eyes were sparkling as if something amusing had been said. "One of my agents stopped it. I may add that it will not be sent."

The ambassador's eyes grew steely, then blank again.

"Mademoiselle, what am I to understand from that?" he demanded.

"You are to understand that I am absolute master of the situation in Washington at this moment," she replied positively. The smile on her lips and the tone of her voice were strangely at variance. "From the beginning I let you understand that ultimately you would receive your instructions from Paris; now I know they will reach you by cable to-morrow. Within a week the compact will be signed. Whether you approve of it or not it will be signed for your country by a special envoy whose authority is greater than yours--his Highness, the Prince Benedetto d'Abruzzi."

"Has he reached Washington?"

"He is in Washington. He has been here for some time, incognito." She was silent a moment. "You have been a source of danger to our plans," she added. "If it had not been for an accident you would still have been comfortably kept out in Alexandria where Mr. Grimm and I found you. Please remember, Monsieur, that we will accomplish what we set out to do. Nothing can stop us--nothing."

At just about the same moment the name of Prince d'Abruzzi had been used in the dining-room, but in a different connection. Mr. Cadwallader was reciting some incident of an automobile trip in Italy when he had been connected with the British embassy there.

"The prince was driving," he said, "and one of the best I ever saw. Corking chap, the prince; democratic, you know, and all that sort of thing. He was one scion of royalty who didn't mind soiling his hands by diving in under a car and fixing it himself. At that time he was inclined to be wild--that was eight or nine years ago--but they say now he has settled down to work, and is one of the real diplomatic powers of Italy. I haven't seen him for a half dozen years."

"How old a man is he?" asked Mr. Grimm carelessly.

"Thirty-five, thirty-eight, perhaps; I don't know," replied Mr. Cadwallader. "It's odd, you know, the number of princes and blue-bloods and all that sort of thing one can find knocking about in Italy and Germany and Spain. One never hears of half of them. I never had heard of the Prince d'Abruzzi until I went to Italy, and I've heard jolly well little of him since, except indirectly."

Mr. Cadwallader lapsed into silence as he sat staring at a large group photograph which was framed on a wall of the dining-room.

"Isn't that the royal family of Italy?" he asked. He rose and went over to it. "By Jove, it is, and here is the prince in the group. The picture was taken, I should say, about the time I knew him."

Mr. Grimm strolled over idly and stood for a long time staring at the photograph.

"He can drive a motor, you know," said Mr. Cadwallader admiringly. "And Italy is the place to drive them. They forgot to make any speed laws over there, and if a chap gets in your way and you knock him silly they arrest him for obstructing traffic, you know. Over here if a chap really starts to go any place in a hurry some bally idiot holds him up."

"Have you ever been held up?" queried Mr. Grimm.

"No, but I expect to be every day," was the reply. "I've got a new motor, you know, and I've never been able to see how fast it is. The other evening I ran up to Baltimore with it in an hour and thirty-seven minutes from Alexandria to Druid Hill Park, and that's better than forty miles. I never did let the motor out, you know, because we ran in the dark most of the way."

Mr. Grimm was still gazing at the photograph.

"Did you go alone?" he asked.

"There's no fun motoring alone, you know. Senorita Rodriguez was with me. Charming girl, what?"

A little while later Mr. Grimm sauntered out into the drawing-room and made his way toward Miss Thorne and the French ambassador. Monsieur Boissegur rose, and offered his hand cordially.

"I hope, Monsieur," said Mr. Grimm, "that you are no worse off for your--your unpleasant experience?"

"Not at all, thanks to you," was the reply. "I have just thanked Miss Thorne for her part in the affair, and--"

"I'm glad to have been of service," interrupted Mr. Grimm lightly.

The ambassador bowed ceremoniously and moved away. Mr. Grimm dropped into the seat he had just left.

"You've left the legation, haven't you?" he asked.

"You drove me out," she laughed.

"Drove you out?" he repeated. "Drove you out?"

"Why, it was not only uncomfortable, but it was rather conspicuous because of the constant espionage of your Mr. Blair and your Mr. Johnson and your Mr. Hastings," she explained, still laughing. "So I have moved to the Hotel Hilliard."

Mr. Grimm was twisting the seal ring on his little finger.

"I'm sorry if I've made it uncomfortable for you," he apologized. "You see it's necessary to--"

"No explanation," Miss Thorne interrupted. "I understand."

"I'm glad you do," he replied seriously. "How long do you intend to remain in the city?"

"Really I don't know--two, three, four weeks, perhaps. Why?"

"I was just wondering."

Senorita Rodriguez came toward them.

"We're going to play bridge," she said, "and we need you, Isabel, to make the four. Come. I hate to take her away, Mr. Grimm."

Mr. Grimm and Miss Thorne rose together. For an instant her slim white hand rested on Mr. Grimm's sleeve and she stared into his eyes understandingly with a little of melancholy in her own. They left Mr. Grimm there.

XVI
LETTERS FROM JAIL

For two weeks Signor Pietro Petrozinni, known to the Secret Service as an unaccredited agent of the Italian government, and the self-confessed assailant of Senor Alvarez of the Mexican legation, had been taking his ease in a cell. He had been formally arraigned and committed without bail to await the result of the bullet wound which had been inflicted upon the diplomatist from Mexico at the German Embassy Ball, and, since then, undisturbed and apparently careless of the outcome, he had spent his time in reading and smoking. He had answered questions with only a curt yes or no when he deigned to answer them at all; and there had been no callers or inquiries for him. He had abruptly declined a suggestion of counsel.

Twice each day, morning and night, he had asked a question of the jailer who brought his simple meals.

"How is Senor Alvarez?"

"He is still in a critical condition." The answer was always the same.

Whereupon the secret agent would return to his reading with not a shadow of uneasiness or concern on his face.

Occasionally there came a courteous little note from Miss Thorne, which he read without emotion, afterward casting them aside or tearing them up. He never answered them. And then one day there came another note which, for no apparent reason, seemed to stir him from his lethargy. Outwardly it was like all the others, but when Signor Petrozinni scanned the sheet his eyes lighted strangely, and he stood staring down at it as though to hide a sudden change of expression in his face. His gaze was concentrated on two small splotches of ink where, it seemed, the pen had scratched as Miss Thorne signed her name.

The guard stood at the barred door for a moment, then started to turn away. The prisoner stopped him with a quick gesture.

"Oh, Guard, may I have a glass of milk, please?" he asked. "No ice. I prefer it tepid."

He thrust a small coin between the bars; the guard accepted it and passed on. Then, still standing at the door, the prisoner read the note again:

"MY DEAR FRIEND:

"I understand, from an indirect source, that there has been a marked improvement in Senor Alvarez's condition, and I am hastening to send you the good news. There is every hope that within a short while, if he continues to improve, we can arrange a bail bond, and you will be free until the time of trial anyway.

"Might it not be well for you to consult an attorney at once? Drop me a line to let me know you received this.

"Sincerely,

"ISABEL THORNE."

Finally the prisoner tossed the note on a tiny table in a corner of his cell, and resumed his reading. After a time the guard returned with the milk.

"Would it be against the rules for me to write an answer to this?" queried Signor Petrozinni, and he indicated the note.

"Certainly not," was the reply.

"If I might trouble you, then, for pen and ink and paper?" suggested the signor and he smiled a little. "Believe me, I would prefer to get them for myself."

"I guess that's right," the guard grinned good-naturedly.

Again he went away and the prisoner sat thoughtfully sipping the milk. He took half of it, then lighted a cigarette, puffed it once or twice and permitted the light to die. After a little there came again the clatter of the guard's feet on the cement pavement, and the writing materials were thrust through the bars.

"Thank you," said the prisoner.

The guard went on, with a nod, and a moment later the signor heard the clangor of a steel door down the corridor as it was closed and locked. He leaned forward in his chair with half-closed eyes, listening for a long time, then rose and noiselessly approached the cell door. Again he listened intently, after which he resumed his seat. He tossed away the cigarette he had and lighted a fresh one, afterward holding the note over the flame of the match. Here and there, where the paper charred in the heat, a letter or word stood out from the bare whiteness of the paper, and finally, a message complete appeared between the innocuous ink-written lines. The prisoner read it greedily:

"Am privately informed there is little chance of Alvarez's recovery. Shall I arrange escape for you, or have ambassador intercede? Would advise former, as the other might take months, and meeting to sign treaty alliance would be dangerously delayed."

Signor Petrozinni permitted the sputtering flame to ignite the paper, and thoughtfully watched the blaze destroy it. The last tiny scrap dropped on the floor, burned out, and he crushed the ashes under his heel. Then he began to write:

"My Dear Miss Thorne:

"Many thanks for your courteous little note. I am delighted to know of the improvement in Senor Alvarez's condition. I had hoped that my impulsive act in shooting him would not end in a tragedy. Please keep me informed of any further change in his condition. As yet I do not see the necessity of consulting an attorney, but later I may be compelled to do so.

"Respectfully,

"Pietro Petrozinni."

This done the secret agent carefully cleaned the ink from the pen, wiping it dry with his handkerchief, then thrust it into the half empty glass of milk. The fluid clung to the steel nib thinly; he went on writing with it, between the lines of ink:

"I am in no danger. I hold credentials to United States, which, when presented, will make me responsible only to the Italian government as special envoy, according to international law. Arrange escape for one week from to-night; use any money necessary. Make careful arrangements for the test and signing of compact for two nights after."

Again the prisoner cleaned the steel nib, after which he put it back in the bottle of ink, leaving it there. He waved the sheet of paper back and forth to dry it, and at last scrutinized it minutely, standing under the light from the high-up window of his cell. Letter by letter the milk evaporated, leaving the sheet perfectly clean and white except for the ink-written message. This sheet he folded, placed in an envelope, and addressed.

Later the guard passed along the corridor, and Signor Petrozinni thrust the letter out to him.

"Be good enough to post that, please," he requested. "It isn't sealed. I don't know if your prison rules require you to read the letters that go out. If so, read it, or have it read, then seal it."

For answer the guard dampened the flap of the envelope, sealed it, thrust it into his pocket and passed on. The secret agent sat down again, and sipped his milk meditatively.

One hour later Mr. Grimm, accompanied by Johnson, came out of a photographer's dark room in Pennsylvania Avenue with a developed negative which he set on a rack to dry. At the end of another hour he was sitting at his desk studying, under a magnifying glass, a finished print of the negative. Word by word he was writing on a slip of paper what his magnifying glass gave him and so, curiously enough, it came to pass that Miss Thorne and Chief Campbell of the Secret Service were reading the hidden, milk-written message at almost the identical moment.

"Johnson got Petrozinni's letter from the postman," Mr. Grimm was explaining. "I opened it, photographed it, sealed it again and remailed it. There was not more than half an hour's delay; and Miss Thorne can not possibly know of it." He paused a moment. "It's an odd thing that writing such as that is absolutely invisible to the naked eye, and yet when photographed becomes decipherable in the negative."

"What do you make of it?" Mr. Campbell asked. The guileless blue eyes were alive with eagerness.

"Well, he's right, of course, about not being in danger," said Mr. Grimm. "If he came with credentials as special envoy this government must respect them, even if Senor Alvarez dies, and leave it to his own government to punish him. If we were officially aware that he has such credentials I doubt if we would have the right to keep him confined; we would merely have to hand him over to the Italian embassy and demand his punishment. And, of course, all that makes him more dangerous than ever."

"Yes, I know that," said the chief a little impatiently. "But who is this man?"

"Who is this man?" Mr. Grimm repeated as if surprised at the question. "I was looking for Prince Benedetto d'Abruzzi, of Italy. I have found him."

Mr. Campbell's clock-like brain ticked over the situation in detail.

"It's like this," Mr. Grimm elucidated. "He has credentials which he knows will free him if he is forced to present them, but I imagine they were given to him more for protection in an emergency like this than for introducing him to our government. As the matter stands he can't afford to discover himself by using those credentials, and yet, if the Latin compact is signed, he must be free. Remember, too, that he is accredited from three countries--Italy, France and Spain." He was silent for a moment. "Naturally his escape from prison would preserve his incognito, and at the same time permit him to sign the compact."

There was silence for a long time.

"I believe the situation is without precedent," said Mr. Campbell slowly. "The special envoy of three great powers held for attempted--!"

"Officially we are not aware of his purpose, or his identity," Mr. Grimm reminded him. "If he escaped it would clarify the situation tremendously."

"If he escaped!" repeated Mr. Campbell musingly.

"But, of course, the compact would not be signed, at least in this country," Mr. Grimm went on tentatively.

Mr. Campbell gazed straight into the listless eyes of the young man for a minute or more, and gradually full understanding came home to him. Finally he nodded his head.

"Use your own judgment, Mr. Grimm," he directed.

XVII
A CALL ON THE WARDEN

The restful silence of night lay over the great prison. Here and there in the grim corridors a guard dozed in the glare of an electric light; and in the office, too, a desk light glimmered where the warden sat at his desk, poring over a report. Once he glanced up at the clock--it was five minutes of eleven--and then he went on with his reading.

After a little the silence was broken by the whir of the clock and the first sharp stroke of the hour; and at just that moment the door from the street opened and a man entered. He was rather tall and slender, and a sinister black mask hid his face from the quickly raised eyes of the warden. For a bare fraction of a second the two men stared at each other, then, instinctively, the warden's right hand moved toward the open drawer of his desk where a revolver lay, and his left toward several electrically connected levers. The intruder noted both gestures, and, unarmed himself, stood silent. The warden was first to speak.

"Well, what is it?"

"You have a prisoner here, Pietro Petrozinni," was the reply, in a pleasant voice. "I have come to demand his release."

The warden's right hand was raised above the desk top, and the revolver in it clicked warningly.

"You have come to demand his release, eh?" he queried. He still sat motionless, with his eyes fixed on the black mask. "How did you pass the outside guard?"

"He was bribed," was the ready response. "Now, Warden," the masked intruder continued pacifically, "it would be much more pleasant all around and there would be less personal danger in it for both of us if you would release Signor Petrozinni without question. I may add that no bribe was offered to you because your integrity was beyond question."

"Thank you," said the warden grimly, "and it shall remain so as long as I have this." He tapped on the desk with the revolver.

"Oh, that isn't loaded," said the masked man quietly.

One quick glance at the weapon showed the warden that the cartridges had been drawn! His teeth closed with a snap at the treachery of it, and with his left hand he pulled back one of the levers--that which should arouse the jailers, turn-keys and guards. Instead of the insistent clangor which he expected, there was silence.

"That wire has been cut," the stranger volunteered.

With clenched teeth the warden pulled the police alarm.

"And that wire was cut, too," the stranger explained.

The warden came to his feet with white face, and nails biting into the palms of his hands. He still held the revolver as he advanced upon the masked man threateningly.

"Not too close, now," warned the intruder, with a sudden hardening of his voice. "Believe me, it would be best for you to release this man, because it must be done, pleasantly or otherwise. I have no desire to injure you, still less do I intend that you shall injure me; and it would be needless for either of us to make a personal matter of it. I want your prisoner, Signor Petrozinni--you will release him at once! That's all!"

The warden paused, dazed, incredulous before the audacity of it, while he studied two calm eyes which peered at him through the slits of the mask.

"And if I *don't* release him?" he demanded at last, fiercely.

"Then I shall take him," was the reply. "It has been made impossible for you to give an alarm," the stranger went on. "The very men on whom you most depended have been bought, and even if they were within sound of your voice now they wouldn't respond. One of your assistants who has been here for years unloaded the revolver in the desk there, and less than an hour ago cut the prison alarm wire. I, personally, cut the police alarm outside the building. So you see!"

As yet there was no weapon in sight, save the unloaded revolver in the warden's hand; at no time had the stranger's voice been raised. His tone was a perfectly normal one.

"Besides yourself there are only five other men employed here who are now awake," the masked man continued. "These are four inner guards and the outer guard. They have all been bought--the turnkeys at five thousand dollars each, and the outer guard at seven thousand. The receipt of all of this money is conditional upon the release of Signor Petrozinni, therefore it is to their interest to aid me as against you. I am telling you all this, frankly and fully, to make you see how futile any resistance would be."

"But who--who is this Signor Petrozinni, that such powerful influences should be brought to bear in his behalf?" demanded the bewildered warden.

"He is a man who can command a vast fortune--and Senor Alvarez is at the point of death. That, I think, makes it clear. Now, if you'll sit down, please!"

"Sit down?" bellowed the warden.

Suddenly he was seized by a violent, maddening rage. He took one step forward and raised the empty revolver to strike. The masked man moved slightly to one side and his clenched fist caught the warden on the point of the chin. The official went down without a sound and lay still, inert. A moment later the door leading into the corridor of the prison opened, and Signor Petrozinni, accompanied by one of the guards, entered the warden's office. The masked man glanced around at them, and with a motion of his head indicated the door leading to the street. They passed through, closing the door behind them.

For a little time the intruder stood staring down at the still body, then he went to the telephone and called police headquarters.

"There has been a jail delivery at the prison," he said in answer to the "hello" of the desk-sergeant at the other end of the wire. "Better send some of your men up to investigate."

"Who is that?" came the answering question.

The stranger replaced the receiver on the hook, stripped off his black mask, dropped it on the floor beside the motionless warden, and went out. It was Mr. Grimm!

XVIII
NOTICE TO LEAVE

At fifteen minutes of midnight when Miss Thorne, followed by Signor Petrozinni, entered the sitting-room of her apartments in the hotel and turned up the light they found Mr. Grimm already there. He rose courteously. At sight of him Miss Thorne's face went deathly white, and the escaped prisoner turned toward the door again.

"I would advise that you stay, your Highness," said Mr. Grimm coldly. Signor Petrozinni paused, amazed. "You will merely subject yourself to the humiliation of arrest if you attempt to leave. The house is guarded by a dozen men."

"Your Highness?" Miss Thorne repeated blankly. "You are assuming a great deal, aren't you, Mr. Grimm?"

"I don't believe," and Mr. Grimm's listless eyes were fixed on those of the escaped prisoner, "I don't believe that Prince Benedetto d'Abruzzi will deny his identity?"

There was one of those long tense silences when eye challenges eye, when wit is pitted against wit, and mind is hauled around to a new, and sometimes unattractive, view of a situation. Miss Thorne stood silent with rigid features, colorless as marble; but slowly a sneer settled about the lips of Signor Petrozinni that was, and he sat down.

"You seem to know everything, Mr. Grimm," he taunted.

"I *try* to know everything, your Highness," was the reply. Mr. Grimm was still standing. "I know, for instance, that one week ago the plot which had your freedom for its purpose was born; I know the contents of every letter that passed between you and Miss Thorne here, notwithstanding the invisible ink; I know that four days ago several thousand dollars was smuggled in to you concealed in a basket of fruit; I know, with that money, you bribed your way out, while Miss Thorne or one of her agents bribed the guard in front; I know that the escape was planned for to-night, and that the man who was delegated to take charge of it is now locked in my office under guard. It may interest you to know that it was I who took his place and made the escape possible. I know that much!"

"You--you--!" the prince burst out suddenly. "You aided me to escape?"

Miss Thorne was staring, staring at them with her eyes widely distended, and her red lips slightly parted.

"Why did you assist him?" she demanded.

"Details are tiresome, Miss Thorne," replied Mr. Grimm with the utmost courtesy. "There is one other thing I know--that the Latin compact will not be signed in the United States."

The prince's eyes met Miss Thorne's inquiringly, and she shook her head. The sneer was still playing about his mouth.

"Anything else of special interest that you know?" he queried.

"Yes, of interest to both you and Miss Thorne. That is merely if the Latin compact is signed anywhere, the English-speaking countries of the world might construe it as a *casus belli* and strike soon enough, and hard enough, to put an end to it once for all."

Again there was silence for a little while. Slowly the prince's eyes were darkening, and a shadow flitted across Miss Thorne's face. The prince rose impatiently.

"Well, what is the meaning of all this? Are you going to take me back to prison?"

"No," said Mr. Grimm. He glanced at his watch. "I will give each of you one-half hour to pack your belongings. We must catch a train at one o'clock."

"Leave the city?" gasped Miss Thorne.

"Impossible!" exclaimed the prince.

"One-half hour," said Mr. Grimm coldly.

"But--but it's out of the question," expostulated Miss Thorne.

"One-half hour," repeated Mr. Grimm. He didn't dare to meet those wonderful blue-gray eyes now. "A special car with private compartments will be attached to the regular train, and the only inconvenience to you will be the fact that the three of us will be compelled to sit up all night. Half a dozen other Secret Service men will be on the train with us."

And then the prince's entire manner underwent a change.

"Mr. Grimm," he said earnestly, "it is absolutely necessary that I remain in Washington for another week--remain here even if I am locked up again--lock me up again if you like. I can't sign compacts in prison."

"Twenty-five minutes," replied Mr. Grimm quietly.

"But here," exclaimed the prince explosively, "I have credentials which will insure my protection in spite of your laws."

"I know that," said Mr. Grimm placidly. "Credentials of that nature can not be presented at midnight, and you will not be here to-morrow to present them. The fact that you have those credentials, your Highness, is one reason why you must leave Washington now, to-night."

XIX
BY WIRELESS

They paused in the office, the three of them, and while Miss Thorne was giving some instructions as to her baggage the prince went over to the telegraph booth and began to write a message on a blank. Mr. Grimm appeared at his elbow.

"No," he said.

"Can't I send a telegram if I like?" demanded the prince sharply.

"No, nor a note, nor a letter, nor may you speak to any one," Mr. Grimm informed him quietly.

"Why, it's an outrage!" flamed the prince.

"It depends altogether on the view-point, your Highness," said Mr. Grimm courteously. "If you will pardon me I might suggest that it is needless to attract attention by your present attitude. You may--I say you *may*--compel me to humiliate you." The prince glared at him angrily. "I mean handcuff you," Mr. Grimm added gratuitously.

"Handcuff *me*?"

"I shouldn't hesitate, your Highness, if it was necessary."

After a moment Miss Thorne signified her readiness, and they started out. At the door Mr. Grimm stopped and turned back to the desk, as if struck by some sudden thought, leaving them together.

"Oh, Miss Thorne left a message for some one," Mr. Grimm was saying to the clerk. "She's decided it is unnecessary." He turned and glanced toward her, and the clerk's eyes followed his. "Please give it to me."

It was passed over without comment. It was a sealed envelope addressed to Mr. Charles Winthrop Rankin. Mr. Grimm glanced at the superscription, tore the envelope into bits and dropped it into a basket. A minute later he was assisting Miss Thorne and the prince into an automobile that was waiting in front. As the car moved away two other automobiles appeared from corners near-by and trailed along behind to the station. There a private compartment-car was in readiness for them.

It was a long, dreary ride--a ride of utter silence save for the roar and clatter of the moving train. Mr. Grimm, vigilant, implacable, sat at ease; Miss Thorne, resigned to the inevitable, whatever it might be, studied the calm, quiet face from beneath drooping lids; and the prince, sullen, scowling, nervously wriggled in his seat. Philadelphia was passed, and Trenton, and then the dawn began to break through the night. It was quite light when they rolled into Jersey City.

"I'm sorry for all the inconvenience I have caused," Mr. Grimm apologized to Miss Thorne as he assisted her to alight. "You must be exhausted."

"If it were only that!" she replied, with a slight smile. "And is it too early to ask where we are going?"

The prince turned quickly at the question.

"We take the ***Lusitania*** for Liverpool at ten o'clock," said Mr. Grimm obligingly. "Meanwhile let's get some coffee and a bite to eat."

"Are you going to make the trip with us?" asked the prince.

Mr. Grimm shrugged his shoulders.

Weary and spiritless they went aboard the boat, and a little while later they steamed out into the stream and threaded their way down the bay. Miss Thorne stood at the rail gazing back upon the city they were leaving. Mr. Grimm stood beside her; the prince, still sullen, still scowling, sat a dozen feet away.

"This is a wonderful thing you have done, Mr. Grimm," said Miss Thorne at last.

"Thank you," he said simply. "It was a destructive thing that you intended to do. Did you ever see a more marvelous thing than that?" and he indicated the sky-line of New York. "It's the most marvelous bit of mechanism in the world; the dynamo of the western hemisphere. You would have destroyed it, because in the world-war that would have been the first point of attack."

She raised her eyebrows, but was silent.

"Somehow," he went on after a moment, "I could never associate a woman with destructiveness, with wars and with violence."

"That is an unjust way of saying it," she interposed. And then, musingly: "Isn't it odd that you and I--standing here by the rail--have, in a way, held the destinies of the whole great earth in our hands? And now your remark makes me feel that you alone have stood for peace and the general good, and I for destruction and evil."

"I didn't mean that," Mr. Grimm said quickly. "You have done your duty as you saw it, and--"

"Failed!" she interrupted.

"And I have done my duty as I saw it."

"And won!" she added. She smiled a little sadly. "I think, perhaps you and I might have been excellent friends if it had not been for all this."

"I know we should have," said Mr. Grimm, almost eagerly. "I wonder if you will ever forgive me for--for--?"

"Forgive you?" she repeated. "There is nothing to forgive. One must do one's duty. But I wish it could have been otherwise."

The Statue of Liberty slid by, and Governor's Island and Fort Hamilton; then, in the distance, Sandy Hook light came into view.

"I'm going to leave you here," said Mr. Grimm, and for the first time there was a tense, strained note in his voice.

Miss Thorne's blue-gray eyes had grown mistily thoughtful; the words startled her a little and she turned to face him.

"It may be that you and I shall never meet again," Mr. Grimm went on.

"We *will* meet again," she said gravely. "When and where I don't know, but it will come."

"And perhaps then we may be friends?" He was pleading now.

"Why, we are friends now, aren't we?" she asked, and again the smile curled her scarlet lips. "Surely we are friends, aren't we?"

"We are," he declared positively.

As they started forward a revenue cutter which had been hovering about Sandy Hook put toward them, flying some signal at her masthead. Slowly the great boat on which they stood crept along, then the clang of a bell in the engine-room brought her to a standstill, and the revenue cutter came alongside.

"I leave you here," Mr. Grimm said again. "It's good-by."

"Good-by," she said softly. "Good-by, till we meet once more."

She extended both hands impulsively and he stood for an instant staring into the limpid gray eyes, then, turning, went below. From the revenue cutter he waved a hand at her as the great *Lusitania*, moving again, sped on her way. The prince joined Miss Thorne at the rail. The scowl was still on his face.

"And now what?" he demanded abruptly. "This man has treated us as if we were a pair of children."

"He's a wonderful man," she replied.

"That may be--but we have been fools to allow him to do all this."

Miss Thorne turned flatly and faced him.

"We are not beaten yet," she said slowly. "If all things go well we--we are not beaten yet."

The *Lusitania* was rounding Montauk Point when the wireless brought her to half-speed with a curt message:

"Isabel Thorne and Pietro Petrozinni aboard *Lusitania* wanted on warrants charging conspiracy. Tug-boat will take them off, intercepting you beyond Montauk Point.

"CAMPBELL, Secret Service."

"What does *that* mean?" asked the prince, bewildered.

"It means that the compact will be signed in Washington in spite of Mr. Grimm," and there was the glitter of triumph in her eyes. "With the aid of one of the maids in the depot at Jersey City I managed to get a telegram of explanation and instruction to De Foe in New York, and this is the result. He signed Mr. Campbell's name, I suppose, to give weight to the message."

An hour later a tug-boat came alongside, and they went aboard.

XX
THE LIGHT IN THE DOME

From where he sat, in a tiny alcove which jutted out and encroached upon the line of the sidewalk, Mr. Grimm looked down on Pennsylvania Avenue, the central thread of Washington, ever changing, always brilliant, splashed at regular intervals with light from high-flung electric arcs. The early theater crowd was in the street, well dressed, well fed, careless for the moment of all things save physical comfort and amusement; automobiles, carriages, cabs, cars flowed past endlessly; and yet Mr. Grimm saw naught of it. In the distance, at one end of the avenue the dome of the capitol cleft the shadows of night, and a single light sparkled at its apex; in the other direction, at the left of the treasury building which abruptly blocks the wide thoroughfare, were the shimmering windows of the White House.

Motionless, moody, thoughtful, Mr. Grimm sat staring, staring straight ahead, comprehending none of these things which lay before him as in a panorama. Instead, his memory was conjuring up a pair of subtle, blue-gray eyes, now pleading, now coquettish, now frankly defiant; two slim, white, wonderful hands; the echo of a pleasant, throaty laugh; a splendid, elusive, radiant-haired phantom. Truly, a woman of mystery! Who was this Isabel Thorne who, for months past, had been the storm-center and directing mind of a vast international intrigue which threatened the world with war? Who, this remarkable young woman who with ease and assurance commanded ambassadors and played nations as pawns?

Now that she was safely out of the country Mr. Grimm had leisure to speculate. Upon him had devolved the duty of blocking her plans, and he had done so--merciless alike of his own feeling and of hers. Hesitation or evasion had never occurred to him. It was a thing to be done, and he did it. He wondered if she had understood, there at the last beside the rail? He wondered if she knew the struggle it had cost him deliberately to send her out of his life? Or had even surmised that her expulsion from the country, by his direct act, was wholly lacking in the exaltation of triumph to him; that it struck deeper than that, below the listless, official exterior, into his personal happiness? And wondering, he knew that she *did* understand.

A silent shod waiter came and placed the coffee things at his elbow. He didn't heed. The waiter poured a demi-tasse, and inquiringly lifted a lump of sugar in the silver tongs. Still Mr. Grimm didn't heed. At last the waiter deposited the sugar on the edge of the fragile saucer, and moved away as silently as he had come. A newspaper which Mr. Grimm had placed on the end of the table when he sat down, rattled a little as a breeze from the open window caught it, then the top sheet slid off and fell to the floor. Mr. Grimm was still staring out the window.

Slowly the room behind him was thinning of its crowd as the theater-bound diners went out in twos and threes. The last of these disappeared finally, and save for Mr. Grimm there were not more than a dozen persons left in the place. Thus for a few minutes, and then the swinging doors leading from the street clicked, and a gentleman entered. He glanced around, as if seeking a seat near a window, then moved along in Mr. Grimm's direction, between the rows of tables. His gaze lingered on Mr. Grimm for an instant, and when he came opposite he stooped and picked up the fallen newspaper sheet.

"Your paper?" he inquired courteously.

Mr. Grimm was still gazing dreamily out of the window.

"I beg pardon," insisted the new-comer pleasantly. He folded the paper once and replaced it on the table. One hand lingered for just the fraction of a moment above Mr. Grimm's coffee-cup.

Aroused by the remark, Mr. Grimm glanced around.

"Oh, thank you," he apologized hastily. "I didn't hear you at first. Thank you."

The new-comer nodded, smiled and passed on, taking a seat two or three tables down. Apparently this trifling courtesy had broken the spell of reverie, for Mr. Grimm squared around to the table again, drew his coffee-cup toward him, and dropped in the single lump of sugar. He idly stirred it for a moment, as his eyes turned again toward the open window, then he lifted the tiny cup and emptied it.

Again he sat motionless for a long time, and thrice the new-comer, only a few feet away, glanced at him narrowly. And now, it seemed, a peculiar drowsiness was overtaking Mr. Grimm. Once he caught himself nodding and raised his head with a jerk. Then he noticed that the arc lights in the street were wobbling curiously, and he fell to wondering why that single flame sparkled at the apex of the capitol dome. Things around him grew hazy, vague, unreal, and then, as if realizing that something was the matter with him, he came to his feet.

He took one step forward into the space between the tables, reeled, attempted to steady himself by holding on to a chair, then everything grew black about him, and he pitched forward on the floor. His face was dead white; his fingers moved a little, nervously, weakly, then they were still.

Several people rose at the sound of the falling body, and the new-comer hurried forward. His coat sleeve caught the empty demi-tasse, as he stooped, and swept it to the floor, where it was shattered. The head waiter and another came, pell-mell, and those diners who had risen came more slowly.

"What's the matter?" asked the head waiter anxiously.

Already the new-comer was supporting Mr. Grimm on his knee, and flicking water in his face.

"Nothing serious, I fancy," he answered shortly. "He's subject to these little attacks."

"What are they? Who is he?"

The stranger tore at Mr. Grimm's collar until it came loose, then he fell to chafing the still hands.

"He is a Mr. Grimm, a government employee--I know him," he answered again. "I imagine it's nothing more serious than indigestion."

A little knot had gathered about them, with offers of assistance.

"Waiter, hadn't you better send for a physician?" some one suggested.

"I'm a physician," the stranger put in impatiently. "Have some one call a cab, and I'll see that he's taken home. It happens that we live in the same apartment house, just a few blocks from here."

Obedient to the crisply-spoken directions, a cab was called, and five minutes later Mr. Grimm, still insensible, was lifted into it. The stranger took a seat beside him, the cabby touched his horse with a whip, and the vehicle fell into the endless, moving line.

XXI
A SLIP OF PAPER

When the light of returning consciousness finally pierced the black lethargy that enshrouded him, Mr. Grimm's mind was a chaos of vagrant, absurd fantasies; then slowly, slowly, realization struggled back to its own, and he came to know things. First was the knowledge that he was lying flat on his back, on a couch, it seemed; then, that he was in the dark--an utter, abject darkness. And finally came an overwhelming sense of silence.

For a while he lay motionless, with not even the movement of an eye-lash to indicate consciousness, wrapped in a delicious languor. Gradually this passed and the feeble flutter of his heart grew into a steady, rhythmic beat. The keen brain was awakening; he was beginning to remember. What had happened? He knew only that in some manner a drug had been administered to him, a bitter dose tasting of opium; that speechlessly, he had fought against it, that he had risen from the table in the restaurant, and that he had fallen. All the rest was blank.

With eyes still closed, and nerveless hands inert at his sides he listened, the while he turned the situation over in speculative mood. The waiter had administered the drug, of course, unless--unless it had been the courteous stranger who had replaced the newspaper on the table! That thought opened new fields of conjecture. Mr. Grimm had no recollection of ever having seen him before; and he had paid only the enforced attention of politeness to him. And why had the drug been administered? Vaguely, incoherently, Mr. Grimm imagined that in some way it had to do with the great international plot of war in which Miss Thorne was so delicate and vital an instrument.

Where was he? Conjecture stopped there. Evidently he was where the courteous gentleman in the restaurant wanted him to be. A prisoner? Probably. In danger? Long, careful attention to detail work in the Secret Service had convinced Mr. Grimm that he was always in danger. That was one reason--and the best--why he had lain motionless, without so much as lifting a finger, since that first glimmer of consciousness had entered his brain. He was probably under scrutiny, even in the darkness, and for the present it was desirable to accommodate any chance watcher by remaining apparently unconscious.

And so for a long time he lay, listening. Was there another person in the room? Mr. Grimm's ears were keenly alive for the inadvertent shuffling of a foot; or the sound of breathing. Nothing. Even the night roar of the city was missing; the silence was oppressive. At last he opened his eyes. A pall of gloom encompassed him--a pall without one rift of light. His fingers, moving slowly, explored the limits of the couch whereon he lay.

Confident, at last, that wherever he was, he was unwatched, Mr. Grimm was on the point of concluding that further inaction was useless, when his straining ears caught the faint grating of metal against metal--perhaps the insertion of a key in the lock. His hands grew still; his eyes closed. And after a moment a door creaked slightly on its hinges, and a breath of cool air informed Mr. Grimm that that open door, wherever it was, led to the outside, and freedom.

There was another faint creaking as the door was shut. Mr. Grimm's nerveless hands closed involuntarily, and his lips were set together tightly. Was it to be a knife thrust in the dark? If not--then what? He expected the flare of a match; instead there was a soft tread, and the rustle of skirts. A woman! Mr. Grimm's caution was all but forgotten in his surprise. As the steps drew nearer his clenched fingers loosened; he waited.

Two hands stretched forward in the dark, touched him simultaneously--one on the face, one on the breast. A singular thrill shot through him, but there was not the flicker of an eye or the twitching of a finger. The woman--it *was* a woman--seemed now to be bending over him, then he heard her drop on her knees beside him, and she pressed an inquiring ear to his left side. It was the heart test.

"Thank God!" she breathed softly.

It was only by a masterful effort that Mr. Grimm held himself limp and inert, for a strange fragrance was enveloping him--a fragrance he well knew.

The hands were fumbling at his breast again, and there was the sharp crackle of paper. At first he didn't understand, then he knew that the woman had pinned a paper to the lapel of his coat. Finally she straightened up, and took two steps away from him, after which came a pause. His keenly attuned ears caught her faint breathing, then the rustle of her skirts as she turned back. She was leaning over him again--her lips touched his forehead, barely; again there was a quick rustling of skirts, the door creaked, and--silence, deep, oppressive, overwhelming silence.

Isabel! Was he dreaming? And then he ceased wondering and fell to remembering her kiss--light as air--and the softly spoken "Thank God!" She did care, then! She *had* understood, that day!

The kiss of a woman beloved is a splendid heart tonic. Mr. Grimm straightened up suddenly on the couch, himself again. He touched the slip of paper which she had pinned to his coat to make sure it was not all a dream, after which he recalled the fact that while he had heard the door creak before she went out he had not heard it creak afterward. Therefore, the door was open. She had left it open. Purposely? That was beside the question at the moment.

And why--how--was she in Washington? Pondering that question, Mr. Grimm's excellent teeth clicked sharply together and he rose. He knew the answer. The compact was to be signed--the alliance which would array the civilized world in arms. He had failed to block that, as he thought. If Miss Thorne had returned, then Prince Benedetto d'Abruzzi, who held absolute power to sign the compact for Italy, France and Spain, had also returned.

Stealthily, feeling his way as he went, Mr. Grimm moved toward the door leading to freedom, guided by the fresh draft of air. He reached the door--it was standing open--and a moment later stepped out into the star-lit night. It was open country here, with a thread of white road just ahead, and farther along a fringe of shrubbery. Mr. Grimm reached the road. Far down it, a pin point in the night, a light flickered through interlacing branches. The tail lamp of an automobile, of course!

Mr. Grimm left the road and skirted a sparse hedge in the direction of the light. After a moment he heard the engine of an automobile, and saw a woman--barely discernible--step into the car. As it started forward he staked everything on one bold move, and won, his reward being a narrow sitting space in the rear of the car, hidden from its occupants by the tonneau. One mile, two miles, three miles they charged through the night, and still he clung on. At last there came relief.

"That's the place, where the lights are--just ahead."

There was no mistaking that voice raised above the clamor of the engine. The car slackened speed, and Mr. Grimm dropped off and darted behind some convenient bushes. And the first thing he did there was to light a match, and read what was written on the slip of paper pinned to his coat. It was, simply:

"My Dear Mr. Grimm:

"By the time you read this the compact will have been signed, and your efforts to prevent it, splendid as they were, futile. It is a tribute to you that it was unanimously agreed that you must be accounted for at the time of the signing, hence the drugging in the restaurant; it was only an act of kindness that I should come here to see that all was well with you, and leave the door open behind me.

"Believe me when I say that you are one man in whom I have never been disappointed. Accept this as my farewell, for now I assume again the name and position rightfully mine. And know, too, that I shall always cherish the belief that you will remember me as

"Your friend,

"ISABEL THORNE.

"P. S. The prince and I left the steamer at Montauk Point, on a tug-boat."

Mr. Grimm kissed the note twice, then burned it.

XXII
THE COMPACT

A room, low-ceilinged, dim, gloomy, sinister as an inquisition chamber; a single large table in the center, holding a kerosene lamp, writing materials and a metal spheroid a shade larger than a one-pound shell; and around it a semicircle of silent, masked and cowled figures. There were twelve of them, eleven men and a woman. In the shadows, which grew denser at the far end of the room, was a squat, globular object, a massive, smooth-sided, black, threatening thing of iron.

One of the men glanced at his watch--it was just two o'clock--then rose and took a position beside the table, facing the semicircle. He placed the timepiece on the table in front of him.

"Gentlemen," he said, and there was the faintest trace of a foreign accent, "I shall speak English because I know that whatever your nationality all of you are familiar with that tongue. And now an apology for the theatric aspect of all this-- the masks, the time and place of meeting, and the rest of it." He paused a moment. "There is only one person living who knows the name and position of all of you," and by a sweep of his hand he indicated the motionless figure of the woman. "It was by her decision that masks are worn, for, while we all know the details of the Latin compact, there is a bare chance that some one will not sign, and it is not desirable that the identity of that person be known to all of us. The reason for the selection of this time and place is obvious, for an inkling of the proposed signing has reached the Secret Service. I will add the United States was chosen as the birthplace of this new epoch in history for several reasons, one being the proximity to Central and South America; and another the inadequate police system which enables greater freedom of action."

He stopped and drew from his pocket a folded parchment. He tapped the tips of his fingers with it from time to time as he talked.

"The Latin compact, gentlemen, is not the dream, of a night, nor of a decade. As long as fifty years ago it was suggested, and whatever differences the Latin countries of the world have had among themselves, they have always realized that ultimately they must stand together against--against the other nations of the world. This idea germinated into action three years ago, and since that time agents have covered the world in its interest. This meeting is the fruition of all that work, and this," he held the parchment aloft, "is the instrument that will unite us. Never has a diplomatic secret been kept as this has been kept; never has a greater reprisal been planned. It means, gentlemen, the domination of the world--socially, spiritually, commercially and artistically; it means that England and the United States, whose sphere of influence has extended around the globe, will be beaten back, that the flag of the Latin countries will wave again over lost possessions. It means all of that, and more."

His voice had risen as he talked until it had grown vibrant with enthusiasm; and his hands pointed his remarks with quick, sharp gestures.

"All this," he went on, "was never possible until three years ago, when the navies of the world were given over into the hands of one nation--my country. Five years ago a fellow-countryman of mine happened to be present at an electrical exhibition in New York City, and there he witnessed an interesting experiment-- practical demonstration of the fact that a submarine mine may be exploded by the use of the Marconi wireless system. He was a practical electrician himself, and the idea lingered in his mind. For two years he experimented, and finally this resulted." He picked up the metal spheroid and held it out for their inspection. "As it stands it is absolutely perfect and gives a world's supremacy to the Latin countries because it places all the navies of the world at our mercy. It is a variation of the well-known percussion cap or fuse by which mines and torpedoes are exploded.

"The theory of it is simple, as are the theories of all great inventions; the secret of its construction is known only to its inventor--a man of whom you never heard. It is merely that the mechanism of the cap is so delicate that the Marconi wireless waves--and *only* those--will fire the cap. In other words, this cap is tuned, if I may use the word, to a certain number of vibrations and half-vibrations; a wireless instrument of high power, with a modifying addition which the inventor has added, has only to be set in motion to discharge it at any distance up to twenty-five miles. High power wireless waves recognize no obstacle, so the explosion of a submarine mine is as easily brought about as would be the explosion of a mine on dry land. You will readily see its value as a protective agency for our seaports."

He replaced the spheroid on the table.

"But its chief value is not in that," he resumed. "Its chief value to the Latin compact, gentlemen, is that the United States and England are now concluding negotiations, unknown to each other, by which *they* will protect *their* seaports by means of mines primed with this cap. The tuning of the caps which we will use is known only to us; *the tuning of the caps which they will use is also known to us*! The addition to the wireless apparatus which they will use is such that they *can not*, even by accident, explode a mine guarding our seaports; but, on the other hand, the addition to the wireless apparatus which *we* will use permits of the extreme high charge which will explode their mines. To make it clearer, we could send a navy against such a city as New York or Liverpool, and explode every mine in front of us as we went; and meanwhile our mines are impervious.

"Another word, and I have finished. Five gentlemen, whom I imagine are present now, have witnessed a test of this cap, by direct command of their home governments. For the benefit of the others of you a simple test has been arranged for to-night. This cap on the table is charged; its inventor is at his wireless instrument, fifteen miles away. At three o'clock he will turn on the current that will explode it." Four of the eleven men looked at their watches. "It is now seventeen minutes past two. I am instructed, for the purposes of the test, to place this cap anywhere you may select--in this house or outside of it, in a box, sealed, or under water. The purpose is merely to demonstrate its efficacy; to prove to your complete satisfaction that it can be exploded under practically any conditions."

His entire manner underwent a change; he drew a chair up to the table, and stood for an instant with his hand resting on the back.

"The compact is written in three languages--English, French and Italian. I shall ask you to sign, after reading either or all, precisely as the directions you have received from your home government instruct. On behalf of the three greatest Latin countries, as special envoy of each, I will sign first."

He dropped into the chair, signed each of the three parchment pages three times, then rose and offered the pen to the cowled figure at one end of the semicir-cle. The man came forward, read the English transcript, studied the three signatures already there with a certain air of surprise, then signed. The second man signed, the third man, and the fourth.

The fifth had just risen to go forward when the door opened silently and Mr. Grimm entered. Without a glance either to right or left, he went straight toward the table, and extended a hand to take the compact.

For an instant there had come amazement, a dumb astonishment, at the intru-sion. It passed, and the hand of the man who had done the talking darted out, seized the compact, and held it behind him.

"If you will be good enough to give that to me, your Highness," suggested Mr. Grimm quietly.

For half a minute the masked man stared straight into the listless eyes of the intruder, and then:

"Mr. Grimm, you are in very grave danger."

"That is beside the question," was the reply. "Be good enough to give me that document."

He backed away as he spoke, kicked the door closed with one heel, then leaned against it, facing them.

"Or better yet," he went on after a moment, "burn it. There is a lamp in front of you." He paused for an answer. "It would be absurd of me to attempt to take it by force," he added.

XXIII
THE PERCUSSION CAP

There was a long, tense silence. The cowled figures had risen ominously; Miss Thorne paled behind her mask, and her fingers gripped her palms fiercely, still she sat motionless. Prince d'Abruzzi broke the silence. He seemed perfectly calm and self-possessed.

"How did you get in?" he demanded.

"Throttled your guard at the front door, took him down cellar and locked him in the coal-bin," replied Mr. Grimm tersely. "I am waiting for you to burn it."

"And how did you escape from--from the other place?"

Mr. Grimm shrugged his shoulders.

"The lamp is in front of you," he said.

"And find your way here?" the prince pursued.

Again Mr. Grimm shrugged his shoulders. For an instant longer the prince gazed straight into his inscrutable face, then turned accusing eyes on the masked figures about him.

"Is there a traitor?" he demanded suddenly. His gaze settled on Miss Thorne and lingered there.

"I can relieve your mind on that point--there is not," Mr. Grimm assured him. "Just a final word, your Highness, if you will permit me. I have heard everything that has been said here for the last fifteen minutes. The details of your percussion cap are interesting. I shall lay them before my government and my government may take it upon itself to lay them before the British government. You yourself said a few minutes ago that this compact was not possible before this cap was invented and perfected. It isn't possible the minute my government is warned against its use. That will be my first duty."

"You are giving some very excellent reasons, Mr. Grimm," was the deliberate reply, "why you should not be permitted to leave this room alive."

"Further," Mr. Grimm resumed in the same tone, "I have been ordered to prevent the signing of that compact, at least in this country. It seems that I am barely in time. If it is signed--and it will be useless now on your own statement unless you murder me--every man who signs it will have to reckon with the highest power of this country. Will you destroy it? I don't want to know what countries already stand committed by the signatures there."

"I will not," was the steady response. And then, after a little: "Mr. Grimm, the inventor of this little cap, insignificant as it seems, will receive millions for it. Your silence would be worth--just how much?"

Mr. Grimm's face turned red, then white again.

"Which would you prefer? An independence by virtue of a great fortune, or--or the other thing?"

Suddenly Miss Thorne tore the mask from her face and came forward. Her cheeks were scarlet, and anger flamed in the blue-gray eyes.

"Mr. Grimm has no price--I happen to know that," she declared hotly. "Neither money nor a consideration for his own personal safety will make him turn traitor." She stared coldly into the prince's eyes. "And we are not assassins here," she added.

"Miss Thorne has stated the matter fairly, I believe, your Highness," and Mr. Grimm permitted his eyes to linger a moment on the flushed face of this woman who, in a way, was defending him. "But there is only one thing to do, Miss Thorne." He was talking to her now. "There is no middle course. It is a problem that has only one possible answer--the destruction of that document, and the departure of you, and you, your Highness, for Italy under my personal care all the way. I imagined this matter had ended that day on the steamer; it *will* end here, now, to-night."

The prince glanced again at his watch, then thoughtfully weighed the percussion cap in his hand, after which, with a curious laugh, he walked over to the squat iron globe in an opposite corner of the room. He bent over it half a minute, then straightened up.

"That cap, Mr. Grimm, has one disadvantage," he remarked casually. "When it is attached to a mine or torpedo it can not be disconnected without firing it. It is attached." He turned to the others. "It is needless to discuss the matter further just now. If you will follow me? We will leave Mr. Grimm here."

With a strange little cry, neither anger nor anguish, yet oddly partaking of the quality of each, Isabel went quickly to the prince.

"How dare you do such a thing?" she demanded fiercely. "It is murder."

"This is not a time, Miss Thorne, for your interference," replied the prince coldly. "It has all passed beyond the point where the feelings of any one person, even the feelings of the woman who has engineered the compact, can be considered. A single life can not be permitted to stand in the way of the consummation of this world project. Mr. Grimm alive means the compact would be useless, if not impossible; Mr. Grimm dead means the fruition of all our plans and hopes. You have done your duty and you have done it well; but now your authority ends, and I, the special envoy of--"

"Just a moment, please," Mr. Grimm interrupted courteously. "As I understand it, your Highness, the mine there in the corner is charged?"

"Yes. It just happened to be here for purposes of experiment."

"The cap is attached?"

"Quite right." The prince laughed.

"And at three o'clock, by your watch, the mine will be fired by a wireless operator fifteen miles from here?"

"Something like that; yes, very much like that," assented the prince.

"Thank you. I merely wanted to understand it." Mr. Grimm pulled a chair up against the door and sat down, crossing his legs. On his knees rested the barrel of a revolver, glittering, fascinating, in the semi-darkness. "Now, gentlemen," and he glanced at his watch, "it's twenty-one minutes of three o'clock. At three that mine will explode. We will all be in the room when it happens, unless his Highness sees fit to destroy the compact."

Eyes sought eyes, and the prince removed his mask with a sudden gesture. His face was bloodless.

"If any man," and Mr. Grimm gave Miss Thorne a quick glance, "I should say, *any person*, attempts to leave this room I *know* he will die; and there's a bare chance that the percussion cap will fail to work. I can account for six of you, if there is a rush."

"But, man, if that mine explodes we shall all be killed--blown to pieces!" burst from one of the cowled figures.

"If the percussion cap works," supplemented Mr. Grimm.

Mingled emotions struggled in the flushed face of Isabel as she studied Mr. Grimm's impassive countenance.

"I have never disappointed you yet, Miss Thorne," he remarked as if it were an explanation. "I shall not now."

She turned to the prince.

"Your Highness, I think it needless to argue further," she said. "We have no choice in the matter; there is only one course--destroy the compact."

"No!" was the curt answer.

"I believe I know Mr. Grimm better than you do," she argued. "You think he will weaken; I know he will not. I am not arguing for him, nor for myself; I am arguing against the frightful loss that will come here in this room if the compact is not destroyed."

"It's absurd to let one man stand in the way," declared the prince angrily.

"It might not be an impertinent question, your Highness," commented Mr. Grimm, "for me to ask how you are going to **prevent** one man standing in the way?"

A quick change came over Miss Thorne's face. The eyes hardened, the lips were set, and lines Mr. Grimm had never seen appeared about the mouth. Here, in a flash, the cloak of dissimulation was cast aside, and the woman stood forth, this keen, brilliant, determined woman who did things.

"The compact will be destroyed," she said.

"No," declared the prince.

"It **must** be destroyed."

"Must? Must? Do you say **must to me?**"

"Yes, **must**," she repeated steadily.

"And by what authority, please, do--"

"By that authority!" She drew a tiny, filigreed gold box from her bosom and cast it upon the table; the prince stared at it. "In the name of your sovereign--must!" she said again.

The prince turned away and began pacing, back and forth across the room with the parchment crumpled in his hand. For a minute or more Isabel stood watching him.

"Thirteen minutes!" Mr. Grimm announced coldly.

And now broke out an excited chatter, a babel of French, English, Italian, Spanish; those masked and cowled ones who had held silence for so long all began talking at once. One of them snatched at the crumpled compact in the prince's hand, while all crowded around him arguing. Mr. Grimm sat perfectly still with the revolver barrel resting on his knees.

"Eleven minutes!" he announced again.

Suddenly the prince turned violently on Miss Thorne with rage-distorted face.

"Do you know what it means to you if I do as you say?" he demanded savagely. "It means you will be branded as traitor, that your name, your property--"

"If you will pardon me, your Highness," she interrupted, "the power that I have used was given to me to use; I have used it. It is a matter to be settled between me and my government, and as far as it affects my person is of no consequence now. You will destroy the compact."

"Nine minutes!" said Mr. Grimm monotonously.

Again the babel broke out.

"Do we understand that you want to see the compact?" one of the cowled men asked suddenly of Mr. Grimm as he turned.

"No, I don't want to see it. I'd prefer not to see it."

With hatred blazing in his eyes the prince made his way toward the lamp, holding a parchment toward the blaze.

"There's nothing else to be done," he exclaimed savagely.

"Just a moment, please," Mr. Grimm interposed quickly. "Miss Thorne, is that the compact?"

She glanced at it, nodded her head, and then the flame caught the fringed edge of paper. It crackled, flashed, flamed, and at last, a thing of ashes, was scattered on the floor. Mr. Grimm rose.

"That is all, gentlemen," he announced courteously. "You are free to go. You, your Highness, and Miss Thorne, will accompany me."

He held open the door and there was almost a scramble to get out. The prince and Miss Thorne waited until the last.

"And, Miss Thorne, if you will give us a lift in your car?" Mr. Grimm suggested. "It is now four minutes of three."

The automobile came in answer to a signal and the three in silence entered it. The car trembled and had just begun to move when Mr. Grimm remembered something, and leaped out.

"Wait for me!" he called. "There's a man locked in the coal-bin!"

He disappeared into the house, and Miss Thorne, with a gasp of horror sank back in her seat with face like chalk. The prince glanced uneasily at his watch, then spoke curtly to the chauffeur.

"Run the car up out of danger; there'll be an explosion there in a moment."

They had gone perhaps a hundred feet when the building they had just left seemed to be lifted bodily from the ground by a great spurt of flame which tore through its center, then collapsed like a thing of cards. The prince, unmoved, glanced around at Miss Thorne; she lay in a dead faint beside him.

"Go ahead," he commanded. "Baltimore."

XXIV
THE PERSONAL EQUATION

Mr. Campbell ceased talking and the deep earnestness that had settled on his face passed, leaving instead the blank, inscrutable mask of benevolence behind which his clock-like genius was habitually hidden. The choleric blue eyes of the president of the United States shifted inquiringly to the thoughtful countenance of the secretary of state at his right, thence along the table around which the official family was gathered. It was a special meeting of the cabinet called at the suggestion of Chief Campbell, and for more than an hour he had done the talking. There had been no interruption.

"So much!" he concluded, at last. "If there is any point I have not made clear Mr. Grimm is here to explain it in person."

Mr. Grimm rose at the mention of his name and stood with his hands clasped behind his back. His eyes met those of the chief executive listlessly.

"We understand, Mr. Grimm," the president began, and he paused for an instant to regard the tall, clean-cut young man with a certain admiration, "we understand that there does not actually exist such a thing as a Latin compact against the English-speaking peoples?"

"On paper, no," was the reply.

"You personally prevented the signing of the compact?"

"I personally caused the destruction of the compact after several signatures had been attached," Mr. Grimm amended. "Throughout I have acted under the direction of Mr. Campbell, of course."

"You were in very grave personal danger?" the president went on.

"It was of no consequence," said Mr. Grimm simply.

The president glanced at Mr. Campbell and the chief shrugged his shoulders.

"You are certain, Mr. Grimm," and the president spoke with great deliberation, "you are certain that the representatives of the Latin countries have not met since and signed the compact?"

"I am not certain--no," replied Mr. Grimm promptly. "I am certain, however, that the backbone of the alliance was broken--its only excuse for existence destroyed--when they permitted me to learn of the wireless percussion cap which would have placed the navies of the world at their mercy. Believe me, gentlemen, if they had kept their secret it would have given them dominion of the earth. They made one mistake," he added in a most matter-of-fact tone. "They should have killed me; it was their only chance."

The president seemed a little startled at the suggestion.

"That would have been murder," he remarked.

"True," Mr. Grimm acquiesced, "but it seems an absurd thing that they should have permitted the life of one man to stand between them and the world power for which they had so long planned and schemed. His Highness, Prince Benedetto d'Abruzzi believed as I do, and so expressed himself." He paused a moment; there was a hint of surprise in his manner. "I expected to be killed, of course. It seemed to me the only thing that could happen."

"They must have known of the far-reaching consequences which would follow upon your escape, Mr. Grimm. Why *didn't* they kill you?"

Mr. Grimm made a little gesture with both hands and was silent.

"May they not yet attempt it?" the president insisted.

"It's too late now," Mr. Grimm explained. "They had everything to gain by killing me there as I stood in the room where I had interrupted the signing of the compact, because that would have been before I had placed the facts in the hands of my government. I was the only person outside of their circle who knew all of them. Only the basest motive could inspire them to attempt my life now."

There was a pause. The secretary of state glanced from Mr. Grimm to Mr. Campbell with a question in his deep-set eyes.

"Do I understand that you placed a Miss Thorne and the prince under--that is, you detained them?" he queried. "If so, where are they now?"

"I don't know," was the reply. "Just before the explosion the three of us entered an automobile together, and then as we were starting away I remembered something which made it necessary for me to reenter the house. When I came out again, just a few seconds before the explosion, the prince and Miss Thorne had gone."

The secretary's lips curled down in disapproval.

"Wasn't it rather unusual, to put it mildly, to leave your prisoners to their own devices that way?" he asked.

"Well, yes," Mr. Grimm admitted. "But the circumstances were unusual. When I entered the house I had locked a man in the cellar. I had to go back to save his life, otherwise--"

"Oh, the guard at the door, you mean?" came the interruption. "Who was it?"

Mr. Grimm glanced at his chief, who nodded.

"It was Mr. Charles Winthrop Rankin of the German embassy," said the young man.

"Mr. Rankin of the German embassy was on guard at the door?" demanded the president quickly.

"Yes. We got out safely."

"And that means that Germany was--!"

The president paused and startled glances passed around the table. After a moment of deep abstraction the secretary went on:

"So Miss Thorne and the prince escaped. Are they still in this country?"

"That I don't know," replied Mr. Grimm. He stood silent a moment, staring at the president. Some subtle change crept into the listless eyes, and his lips were set. "Perhaps I had better explain here that the personal equation enters largely into an affair of this kind," he said at last, slowly. "It happens that it entered into this. Unless I am ordered to pursue the matter further I think it would be best for all concerned to accept the fact of Miss Thorne's escape, and--" He stopped.

There was a long, thoughtful silence. Every man in the room was studying Mr. Grimm's impassive face.

"Personal equation," mused the president. "Just how, Mr. Grimm, does the personal equation enter into the affair?"

The young man's lips closed tightly, and then:

"There are some people, Mr. President, whom we meet frankly as enemies, and we deal with them accordingly; and there are others who oppose us and yet are not enemies. It is merely that our paths of duty cross. We may have the greatest respect for them and they for us, but purposes are unalterably different. In other words there is a personal enmity and a political enmity. You, for instance, might be a close personal friend of the man whom you defeated for president. There might"--he stopped suddenly.

"Go on," urged the president.

"I think every man meets once in his life an individual with whom he would like to reckon personally," the young man continued. "That reckoning may not be a severe one; it may be less severe than the law would provide; but it would be a personal reckoning. There is one individual in this affair with whom I should like to reckon, hence the personal equation enters very largely into the case."

For a little while the silence of the room was unbroken, save for the steady tick-tock of a great clock in one corner. Mr. Grimm's eyes were fixed unwaveringly upon those of the chief executive. At last the secretary of war crumpled a sheet of paper impatiently and hitched his chair up to the table.

"Coming down to the facts it's like this, isn't it?" he demanded briskly. "The Latin countries, by an invention of their own which the United States and England were to be duped into purchasing, would have had power to explode every submarine mine before attacking a port? Very well. This thing, of course, would have given them the freedom of the seas as long as we were unable to explode their submarines as they were able to explode ours. And this is the condition which made the Latin compact possible, isn't it?"

He looked straight at Mr. Grimm, who nodded.

"Therefore," he went on, "if the Latin compact is not a reality on paper; if the United States and England do not purchase this--this wireless percussion cap, we are right back where we were before it all happened, aren't we? Every possible danger from that direction has passed, hasn't it? The world-war of which we have been talking is rendered impossible, isn't it?"

"That's a question," answered Mr. Grimm. "If you will pardon me for suggesting it, I would venture to say that as long as there is an invention of that importance in the hands of nations whom we now know have been conspiring against us for fifty years, there is always danger. It seems to me, if you will pardon me again, that for the sake of peace we must either get complete control of that invention or else understand it so well that there can be no further danger. And again, please let me call your attention to the fact that the brain which brought this thing into existence is still to be reckoned with. There may, some day, come a time when our submarines may be exploded at will regardless of this percussion cap."

The secretary of war turned flatly upon Chief Campbell.

"This woman who is mixed up in this affair?" he demanded. "This Miss Thorne. Who is she?"

"Who is she?" repeated the chief. "She's a secret agent of Italy, one of the most brilliant, perhaps, that has ever operated in this or any other country. She is the pivot around which the intrigue moved. We know her by a dozen names; any one of them may be correct."

The brows of the secretary of war were drawn down in thought as he turned to the president.

"Mr. Grimm was speaking of the personal equation," he remarked pointedly. "I think perhaps his meaning is clear when we know there is a woman in the case. We know that Mr. Grimm has done his duty to the last inch in this matter; we know that alone and unaided, practically, he has done a thing that no living man of his relative position has ever done before--prevented a world-war. But there is further danger--he himself has called our attention to it--therefore, I would suggest that Mr. Grimm be relieved of further duty in this particular case. This is not a moment when the peace of the world may be imperiled by personal feelings of--of kindliness for an individual."

Mr. Grimm received the blow without a tremor. His hands were still idly clasped behind his back; the eyes fastened upon the president's face were still listless; the mouth absolutely without expression.

"As Mr. Grimm has pointed out," the secretary went on, "we have been negotiating for this wireless percussion cap. I have somewhere in my office the name and address of the individual with whom these negotiations have been conducted. Through that it is possible to reach the inventor, and then--! I suggest that we vote our thanks to Mr. Grimm and relieve him of this particular case."

The choleric eyes of the president softened a little, and grew grave as they studied the impassive face of the young man.

"It's a strange situation, Mr. Grimm," he said evenly. "What do you say to withdrawing?"

"I am at your orders, Mr. President," was the reply.

"No one knows better what you have done than the gentlemen here at this table," the president went on slowly. "No one questions that you have done more than any other man could have done under the circumstances. We understand, I think, that indirectly you are asking immunity for an individual. I don't happen to know the liability of that individual under our law, but we can't make any mistake now, Mr. Grimm, and so--and so--" He stopped and was silent.

"I had hoped, Mr. President, that what I have done so far--and I don't underestimate it--would have, at least, earned for me the privilege of remaining in this case until its conclusion," said Mr. Grimm steadily. "If it is to be otherwise, of course I am at--"

"History tells us, Mr. Grimm," interrupted the president irrelevantly, "that the frou-frou of a woman's skirt has changed the map of the world. Do you believe," he went on suddenly, "that a man can mete out justice fairly, severely if necessary, to one for whom he has a personal regard?"

"I do, sir."

"Perhaps even to one--to a woman whom he might love?"

"I do, sir."

The president rose.

"Please wait in the anteroom for a few minutes," he directed.

Mr. Grimm bowed himself out. At the end of half an hour he was again summoned into the cabinet chamber. The president met him with outstretched hand. There was more than mere perfunctory thanks in this--there was the understanding of man and man.

"You will proceed with the case to the end, Mr. Grimm," he instructed abruptly. "If you need assistance ask for it; if not, proceed alone. You will rely upon your own judgment entirely. If there are circumstances which make it inadvisable to move against an individual by legal process, even if that individual is amenable to our laws, you are not constrained so to do if your judgment is against it. There is one stipulation: You will either secure the complete rights of the wireless percussion cap to this government or learn the secret of the invention so that at no future time can we be endangered by it."

"Thank you," said Mr. Grimm quietly. "I understand."

"I may add that it is a matter of deep regret to me," and the president brought one vigorous hand down on the young man's shoulder, "that our government has so few men of your type in its service. Good day."

XXV
WE TWO

Mr. Grimm turned from Pennsylvania Avenue into a cross street, walked along half a block or so, climbed a short flight of stairs and entered an office.

"Is Mr. Howard in?" he queried of a boy in attendance.

"Name, please."

Mr. Grimm handed over a sealed envelope which bore the official imprint of the Department of War in the upper left hand corner; and the boy disappeared into a room beyond. A moment later he emerged and held open the door for Mr. Grimm. A gentleman--Mr. Howard--rose from his seat and stared at him as he entered.

"This note, Mr. Grimm, is surprising," he remarked.

"It is only a request from the secretary of war that I be permitted to meet the inventor of the wireless percussion cap," Mr. Grimm explained carelessly. "The negotiations have reached a point where the War Department must have one or two questions answered directly by the inventor. Simple enough, you see."

"But it has been understood, and I have personally impressed it upon the secretary of war that such a meeting is impossible," objected Mr. Howard. "All negotiations have been conducted through me, and I have, as attorney for the inventor, the right to answer any question that may properly be answered. This now is a request for a personal interview with the inventor."

"The necessity for such an interview has risen unexpectedly, because of a pressing need of either closing the deal or allowing it to drop," Mr. Grimm stated. "I may add that the success of the deal depends entirely on this interview."

Mr. Howard was leaning forward in his chair with wrinkled brow intently studying the calm face of the young man. Innocent himself of all the intrigue and international chicanery back of the affair, representing only an individual in these secret negotiations, he saw in the statement, as Mr. Grimm intended that he should, the possible climax of a great business contract. His greed was aroused; it might mean hundreds of thousands of dollars to him.

"Do you think the deal can be made?" he asked at last.

"I have no doubt there will be some sort of a deal," replied Mr. Grimm. "As I say, however, it is absolutely dependent on an interview between the inventor and myself at once--this afternoon."

Mr. Howard thoughtfully drummed on his desk for a little while. From the first, save in so far as the patent rights were concerned, he had seen no reasons for the obligations of utter secrecy which had been enforced upon him. Perhaps, if he laid it before the inventor in this new light, with the deal practically closed, the interview would be possible!

"I have no choice in the matter, Mr. Grimm," he said at last. "I shall have to put it to my client, of course. Can you give me, say, half an hour to communicate with him?"

"Certainly," and Mr. Grimm rose obligingly. "Shall I wait outside here or call again?"

"You may wait if you don't mind," said Mr. Howard. "I'll be able to let you know in a few minutes, I hope."

Mr. Grimm bowed and passed out. At the end of twenty-five minutes the door of Mr. Howard's private office opened and he appeared. His face was violently red, evidently from anger, and perspiration stood on his forehead.

"I can't do anything with him," he declared savagely. "He says simply that negotiations must be conducted through me or not at all."

Mr. Grimm had risen; he bowed courteously.

"Very well," he said placidly. "You understand, of course, as the note says, that this refusal of his terminates the negotiations, so--"

"But just a moment--" interposed Mr. Howard quickly.

"Good day," said Mr. Grimm.

The door opened and closed; he was gone. Three minutes later he stepped into a telephone booth at a near-by corner and took down the receiver.

"Hello, central!" he called, and then: "This is Mr. Grimm of the Secret Service.

What number was Mr. Howard talking to?"

"Eleven double-nought six, Alexandria," was the reply.

"Where is the connection? In whose name?"

"The connection is five miles out from Alexandria in a farm-house on the old Baltimore Road," came the crisp, business-like answer. "The name is Murdock Williams."

"Thank you," said Mr. Grimm. "Good-by."

A moment later he was standing by the curb waiting for a car, when Howard, still angry, and with an expression of deep chagrin on his face, came bustling up.

"If you can give me until to-morrow afternoon, then--" he began.

Mr. Grimm glanced around at him, and with a slight motion of his head summoned two men who had been chatting near-by. One of them was Blair, and the other Hastings.

"Take this man in charge," he directed. "Hold him in solitary confinement until you hear from me. Don't talk to him, don't let any one else talk to him, and don't let him talk. If any person speaks to him before he is locked up, take that person in charge also. He is guilty of no crime, but a single word from him now will endanger my life."

That was all. It was said and done so quickly that Howard, dazed, confused and utterly unable to account for anything, was led away without a protest. Mr. Grimm, musing gently on the stupidity of mankind in general and the ease with which it is possible to lead even a clever individual into a trap, if the bait appeals to greed, took a car and went up town.

Some three hours later he walked briskly along a narrow path strewn with pine needles, which led tortuously up to an old colonial farmhouse. Outwardly the place seemed to be deserted. The blinds, battered and stripped of paint by wind and rain, were all closed and one corner of the small veranda had crumbled away from age and neglect. In the rear of the house, rising from an old barn, a thin pole with a cup-like attachment at the apex, thrust its point into the open above the dense, odorous pines. Mr. Grimm noted these things as he came along.

He stepped up quietly on the veranda and had just extended one hand to rap on the door when it was opened from within, and Miss Thorne stood before him. He was not surprised; intuition had told him he would meet her again, perhaps here in hiding. A sudden quick tenderness lighted the listless eyes. For an instant she stood staring, her face pallid against the gloom of the hallway beyond, and she drew a long breath of relief, as she pressed one hand to her breast. The blue-gray eyes were veiled by drooping lids, then she recovered herself and they opened into his. In them he saw anxiety, apprehension, fear even.

"Miss Thorne!" he greeted, and he bowed low over the white hand which she impulsively thrust toward him.

"I--I knew some one was coming," she stammered in a half whisper. "I didn't know it was you; I hadn't known definitely until this instant that you were safe from the explosion. I am glad--glad, you understand; glad that you were not--" She stopped and fought back her emotions, then went on: "But you must not come in; you must go away at once. Your--your life is in danger here."

"How did you know I was coming?" inquired Mr. Grimm.

"From the moment Mr. Howard telephoned," she replied, still hastily, still in the mysterious half whisper. "I knew that it could only be some one from your bureau, and I hoped that it was you. I saw how you forced him to call us up here, and that was all you needed. It was simple, of course, to trace the telephone call." Both of her hands closed over one of his desperately. "Now, go, please. The Latin compact is at an end; you merely invite death here. Now, go!"

Her eyes were searching the listless face with entreaty in them; the slender fingers were fiercely gripping one of Mr. Grimm's nerveless hands. For an instant some strange, softening light flickered in the young man's eyes, then it passed.

"I have no choice, Miss Thorne," he said gravely at last. "I am honor bound by my government to do one of two things. If I fail in the first of those--the greater--it can only be because--"

He stopped; hope flamed up in her eyes and she leaned forward eagerly studying the impassive face.

"Because--?" she repeated.

"It can only be because I am killed," he added quietly. Suddenly his whole manner changed. "I should like to see the--the inventor?"

"But don't you see--don't you see you *will* be killed if--?" she began tensely.

"May I see the inventor, please?" Mr. Grimm interrupted.

For a little time she stood, white and rigid, staring at him. Then her lids fluttered down wearily, as if to veil some crushing agony within her, and she stepped aside. Mr. Grimm entered and the door closed noiselessly behind him. After a moment her hand rested lightly on his arm, and he was led into a room to his left. This door, too, she closed, immediately turning to face him.

"We may talk here a few minutes without interruption," she said in a low tone. Her voice was quite calm now. "If you will be--?"

"Please understand, Miss Thorne," he interposed mercilessly, "that I must see the inventor, whoever he is. What assurance have I that this is not some ruse to permit him to escape?"

"You have my word of honor," she said quite simply.

"Please go on." He sat down.

"You will see him too soon, I fear," she continued slowly. "If you had not come to him he would have gone to you." She swayed a little and pressed one hand to her eyes. "I would to God it were in my power to prevent that meeting!" she exclaimed desperately. Then, with an effort: "There are some things I want to explain to you. It may be that you will be willing to go then of your own free will. If I lay bare to you every step I have taken since I have been in Washington; if I make clear to you every obscure point in this hideous intrigue; if I confess to you that the Latin compact has been given up for all time, won't that be enough? Won't you go then?"

Mr. Grimm's teeth closed with a snap.

"I don't want that--from you," he declared.

"But if I should tell it all to you?" she pleaded.

"I won't listen, Miss Thorne. You once paid me the compliment of saying that I was one man you knew in whom you had never been disappointed." The listless eyes were blazing into her own now. "I have never been disappointed in you. I will not permit you to disappoint me now. The secrets of your government are mine if I can get them--but I won't allow you to tell them to me."

"My government!" Miss Thorne repeated, and her lips curled sadly. "I--I have no government. I have been cast off by that government, stripped of my rank, and branded as a traitor!"

"Traitor!" Mr. Grimm's lips formed the word silently.

"I failed, don't you see?" she rushed on. "Ignominy is the reward of failure. Prince d'Abruzzi went on to New York that night, cabled a full account of the destruction of the compact to my government, and sailed home on the following day. I was the responsible one, and now it all comes back on me." For a moment she was silent. "It's so singular, Mr. Grimm. The fight from the first was between us--we two; and you won."

XXVI
IN WHICH THEY BOTH WIN

Mr. Grimm dropped into a chair with his teeth clenched, and his face like chalk. For a minute or more he sat there turning it all over in his mind. Truly the triumph had been robbed of its splendor when the blow fell here--here upon a woman he loved.

"There's no shame in the confession of one who is fairly beaten," Isabel went on softly, after a little. "There are many things that you don't understand. I came to Washington with an authority from my sovereign higher even than that vested in the ambassador; I came *as* I did and compelled Count di Rosini to obtain an invitation to the state ball for me in order that I might meet a representative of Russia there that night and receive an answer as to whether or not they would join the compact. I received that answer; its substance is of no consequence now.

"And you remember where I first met you? It was while you were investigating the shooting of Senor Alvarez in the German embassy. That shooting, as you know, was done by Prince d'Abruzzi, so almost from the beginning my plans went wrong because of the assumption of authority by the prince. The paper he took from Senor Alvarez after the shooting was supposed to bear vitally upon Mexico's attitude toward our plan, but, as it developed, it was about another matter entirely."

"Yes, I know," said Mr. Grimm.

"The event of that night which you did *not* learn was that Germany agreed to join the compact upon conditions. Mr. Rankin, who was attached to the German embassy in an advisory capacity, delivered the answer to me, and I pretended to faint in order that I might reasonably avoid you."

"I surmised that much," remarked Mr. Grimm.

"The telegraphing I did with my fan was as much to distract your attention as anything else, and at the same time to identify myself to Mr. Rankin, whom I had never met. You knew him, of course; I didn't."

She was silent a while as her eyes steadily met those of Mr. Grimm. Finally she went on:

"When next I met you it was in the Venezuelan legation; you were investigating the theft of the fifty thousand dollars in gold from the safe. I thrust myself into that case, because I was afraid of you; and mercilessly destroyed a woman's name in your eyes to further my plans. I made you believe that Senorita Rodriguez stole that fifty thousand dollars, and I returned it to you, presumably, while we stood in her room that night. Only it was not her room--it was *mine! I* stole the fifty thousand dollars! All the details, even to her trip to see Mr. Griswold in Baltimore in company with Mr. Cadwallader, had been carefully worked out; and she *did* bring me the combination of the safe from Mr. Griswold on the strength of a forged letter. But she didn't know it. There was no theft, of course. I had no intention of keeping the money. It was necessary to take it to distract attention from the thing I *did* do--break a lock inside the safe to get a sealed packet that contained Venezuela's answer to our plan. I sealed that packet again, and there was never a suspicion that it had been opened."

"Only a suspicion," Mr. Grimm corrected.

"Then came the abduction of Monsieur Boissegur, the French ambassador. I plunged into that case as I did in the other because I was afraid of you and had to know just how much you knew. It was explained to you as an attempt at extortion with details which I carefully supplied. As a matter of fact, Monsieur Boissegur opposed our plans, even endangered them; and it was not advisable to have him recalled or even permit him to resign at the moment. So we abducted him, intending to hold him until direct orders could reach him from Paris. Understand, please, that all these things were made possible by the aid and cooperation of dozens, scores, of agents who were under my orders; every person who appeared in that abduction was working at my direction. The ambassador's unexpected escape disarranged our plans; but he was taken out of the embassy by force the second time under your very eyes. The darkness which made this possible was due to the fact that while you were looking for the switch, and I was apparently aiding, I was holding my hand over it all the time to keep you from turning on the light. You remember that?"

Mr. Grimm nodded.

"All the rest of it you know," she concluded wearily. "You compelled me to leave the Venezuelan legation by your espionage, but in the crowded hotel to which I moved I had little difficulty avoiding your Mr. Hastings, your Mr. Blair and your Mr. Johnson, so I came and went freely without your knowledge. The escape of the prince from prison you arranged, so you understand all of that, as well as the meeting and attempted signing of the compact, and the rapid recovery of Senor Alvarez. And, after all, it was my fault that our plans failed, because if I had not been--been uneasy as to your condition and had not made the mistake of going to the deserted little house where you were a prisoner, the plans would have succeeded, the compact been signed."

"I'm beginning to understand," said Mr. Grimm gravely, and a wistful, tender look crept into his eyes. "If it had not been for that act of--consideration and kindness to me--"

"We would have succeeded in spite of you," explained Isabel. "We were afraid of you, Mr. Grimm. It was a compliment to you that we considered it necessary to account for your whereabouts at the time of the signing of the compact."

"And if you had succeeded," remarked Mr. Grimm, "the whole civilized world would have come to war."

"I never permitted myself to think of it that way," she replied frankly. "There is something splendid to me in a battle of brains; there is exaltation, stimulation, excitement in it. It has always possessed the greatest fascination for me. I have always won, you know, until now. I failed! And my reward is 'Traitor!'"

"Just a word of assurance now," she went on after a moment. "The Latin compact has been definitely given up; the plan has been dismissed, thanks to you; the peace of the world is unbroken. And who am I? I know you have wondered; I know your agents have scoured the world to find out. I am the daughter of a former Italian ambassador to the Court of St. James. My mother was an English woman. I was born and received my early education in England, hence my perfect knowledge of that tongue. In Rome I am, or have been, alas, the Countess Rosa d'Orsetti; now I am an exile with a price on my head. That is all, except for several years I was a trusted agent of my government, and a friend of my queen."

She rose and extended both hands graciously. Mr. Grimm seized the slender white fingers and stood with eyes fixed upon hers. Slowly a flush crept into her pallid cheeks, and she bowed her head.

"Wonderful woman!" he said softly.

"I shall ask a favor of you now," she went on gently. "Let all this that you have learned take the place of whatever you expected to learn, and go. Believe me, there can only be one result if you meet--if you meet the inventor of the wireless cap upon which so much was staked, and so much lost." She shuddered a little, then raised the blue-gray eyes beseechingly to his face. "Please go."

Go! The word straightened Mr. Grimm in his tracks and he allowed her hands to fall limply. Suddenly his face grew hard. In the ecstasy of adoration he had momentarily forgotten his purpose here. His eyes lost their ardor; his nerveless hands dropped beside him.

"No," he said.

"You must--you must," she urged gently. "I know what it means to you. You feel it your duty to unravel the secret of the percussion cap? You can't; no man can. No one knows the inventor more intimately than I, and even I couldn't get it from him. There are no plans for it in existence, and even if there were he would no more sell them than you would have accepted a fortune at the hands of Prince d'Abruzzi to remain silent. The compact has failed; you did that. The agents have scattered-- gone to other duties. That is enough."

"No," said Mr. Grimm. There was a strange fear tearing at his heart,--"No one knows the inventor more intimately than I." "No," he said again. "I won from my government a promise to be made good upon a condition--I must fulfil that condition."

"But there is nothing, promotion, honor, reward, that would compensate you for the loss of your life," she entreated. "There is still time." She was pleading now, with her slim white hands resting on his shoulders, and the blue-gray eyes fixed upon his face.

"It's more than all that," he said. "That condition is you--your safety."

"For me?" she repeated. "For me? Then, won't you go for--for my sake?"

"No."

"Won't you go if you know you will be killed," and suddenly her face turned scarlet, "and that your life is dear to me?"

"No."

Isabel dropped upon her knees before him.

"This inventor--this man whom you insist on seeing is half insane with disappointment and anger," she rushed on desperately. "Remember that a vast fortune, honor, fame were at his finger tips when you--you placed them beyond his reach by the destruction of the compact. He has sworn to kill you."

"I can't go!"

"If you *know* that when you meet one of you will die?"

"No." The answer came fiercely, through clenched teeth. Mr. Grimm disengaged his right hand and drew his revolver; the barrel clicked under his fingers as it spun.

"If I tell you that of the two human beings in this world whom I love this man is one?"

"No."

A shuffling step sounded in the hallway just outside. Mr. Grimm stepped back from the kneeling figure, and turned to face the door with his revolver ready.

"Great God!" It was a scream of agony. "He is my brother! Don't you see?"

She came to her feet and went staggering across to the door. The key clicked in the lock.

"Your brother!" exclaimed Mr. Grimm.

"He wouldn't listen to me--you wouldn't listen to me, and now--and *now*! God have mercy!"

There was a sharp rattling, a clamor at the door, and Isabel turned to Mr. Grimm mutely, with arms outstretched. The revolver barrel clicked under his hand, then, after a moment, he replaced the weapon in his pocket.

"Please open the door," he requested quietly.

"He'll kill you!" she screamed.

Exhausted, helpless, she leaned against a chair with her face in her hands. Mr. Grimm went to her suddenly, tore the hands from her face, and met the tear-stained eyes.

"I love you," he said. "I want you to know that!"

"And I love you--that's why it matters so."

Leaving her there, Mr. Grimm strode straight to the door and threw it open. He saw only the outline of a thin little man of indeterminate age, then came a blinding flash under his eyes, and he leaped forward. There was a short, sharp struggle, and both went down. The revolver! He must get that! He reached for it with the one idea of disarming this madman. The muzzle was thrust toward him, he threw up his arm to protect his head, and then came a second flash. Instantly he felt the figure in his arms grow limp; and after a moment he rose. The face of the man on the floor was pearly gray; and a thin, scarlet thread flowed from his temple.

He turned toward Isabel. She lay near the chair, a little crumpled heap. In a stride he was beside her, and had lifted her head to his knee. The blue-gray eyes opened into his once, then they closed. She had fainted. The first bullet had pierced her arm; it was only a flesh wound. He lifted her gently and placed her on a couch, after which he disappeared into another room. In a little while there came the cheerful ting-a-ling of a telephone bell.

"Is this the county constable's office?" he inquired. "Well, there's been a little shooting accident at the Murdock Williams' place, five miles out from Alexandria on the old Baltimore Road. Please send some of your men over to take charge. Two hours from now call up Mr. Grimm at Secret Service headquarters in Washington and he will explain. Good-by."

And a few minutes later Mr. Grimm walked along the road toward an automobile a hundred yards away, bearing Miss Thorne in his arms. The chauffeur cranked the machine and climbed to his seat.

"Washington!" directed Mr. Grimm. "Never mind the speed laws."

The Codes Of Hammurabi And Moses
W. W. Davies

QTY

The discovery of the Hammurabi Code is one of the greatest achievements of archaeology, and is of paramount interest, not only to the student of the Bible, but also to all those interested in ancient history...

Religion   ISBN: *1-59462-338-4*   **Pages:132**

MSRP $12.95

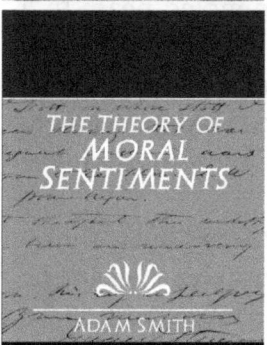

The Theory of Moral Sentiments
Adam Smith

QTY

This work from 1749. contains original theories of conscience amd moral judgment and it is the foundation for systemof morals.

Philosophy   ISBN: *1-59462-777-0*   **Pages:536**

MSRP $19.95

Jessica's First Prayer
Hesba Stretton

QTY

In a screened and secluded corner of one of the many railway-bridges which span the streets of London there could be seen a few years ago, from five o'clock every morning until half past eight, a tidily set-out coffee-stall, consisting of a trestle and board, upon which stood two large tin cans, with a small fire of charcoal burning under each so as to keep the coffee boiling during the early hours of the morning when the work-people were thronging into the city on their way to their daily toil...

Pages:84

Childrens   ISBN: *1-59462-373-2*   *MSRP $9.95*

My Life and Work
Henry Ford

QTY

Henry Ford revolutionized the world with his implementation of mass production for the Model T automobile. Gain valuable business insight into his life and work with his own auto-biography... "We have only started on our development of our country we have not as yet, with all our talk of wonderful progress, done more than scratch the surface. The progress has been wonderful enough but..."

Pages:300

Biographies/   ISBN: *1-59462-198-5*   *MSRP $21.95*

The Art of Cross-Examination
Francis Wellman

QTY

I presume it is the experience of every author, after his first book is published upon an important subject, to be almost overwhelmed with a wealth of ideas and illustrations which could readily have been included in his book, and which to his own mind, at least, seem to make a second edition inevitable. Such certainly was the case with me; and when the first edition had reached its sixth impression in five months, I rejoiced to learn that it seemed to my publishers that the book had met with a sufficiently favorable reception to justify a second and considerably enlarged edition. ..

Reference   ISBN: *1-59462-647-2*

Pages:412

MSRP $19.95

On the Duty of Civil Disobedience
Henry David Thoreau

QTY

Thoreau wrote his famous essay, On the Duty of Civil Disobedience, as a protest against an unjust but popular war and the immoral but popular institution of slave-owning. He did more than write—he declined to pay his taxes, and was hauled off to gaol in consequence. Who can say how much this refusal of his hastened the end of the war and of slavery ?

Law   ISBN: *1-59462-747-9*

Pages:48

MSRP $7.45

Dream Psychology Psychoanalysis for Beginners
Sigmund Freud

QTY

Sigmund Freud, born Sigismund Schlomo Freud (May 6, 1856 - September 23, 1939), was a Jewish-Austrian neurologist and psychiatrist who co-founded the psychoanalytic school of psychology. Freud is best known for his theories of the unconscious mind, especially involving the mechanism of repression; his redefinition of sexual desire as mobile and directed towards a wide variety of objects; and his therapeutic techniques, especially his understanding of transference in the therapeutic relationship and the presumed value of dreams as sources of insight into unconscious desires.

Dream Psychology
Psychoanalysis for Beginners

Sigmund Freud

Psychology   ISBN: *1-59462-905-6*

Pages:196

MSRP $15.45

The Miracle of Right Thought
Orison Swett Marden

QTY

Believe with all of your heart that you will do what you were made to do. When the mind has once formed the habit of holding cheerful, happy, prosperous pictures, it will not be easy to form the opposite habit. It does not matter how improbable or how far away this realization may see, or how dark the prospects may be, if we visualize them as best we can, as vividly as possible, hold tenaciously to them and vigorously struggle to attain them, they will gradually become actualized, realized in the life. But a desire, a longing without endeavor, a yearning abandoned or held indifferently will vanish without realization.

Pages:360

Self Help   ISBN: *1-59462-644-8*

MSRP $25.45

QTY

The Rosicrucian Cosmo-Conception Mystic Christianity *by Max Heindel*   ISBN: *1-59462-188-8*   **$38.95**
The Rosicrucian Cosmo-conception is not dogmatic, neither does it appeal to any other authority than the reason of the student. It is: not controversial, but is: sent forth in the, hope that it may help to clear...   New Age/Religion Pages 646

Abandonment To Divine Providence *by Jean-Pierre de Caussade*   ISBN: *1-59462-228-0*   **$25.95**
"The Rev. Jean Pierre de Caussade was one of the most remarkable spiritual writers of the Society of Jesus in France in the 18th Century. His death took place at Toulouse in 1751. His works have gone through many editions and have been republished...   Inspirational/Religion Pages 400

Mental Chemistry *by Charles Haanel*   ISBN: *1-59462-192-6*   **$23.95**
Mental Chemistry allows the change of material conditions by combining and appropriately utilizing the power of the mind. Much like applied chemistry creates something new and unique out of careful combinations of chemicals the mastery of mental chemistry...   New Age Pages 354

The Letters of Robert Browning and Elizabeth Barret Barrett 1845-1846 vol II   ISBN: *1-59462-193-4*   **$35.95**
by Robert Browning and Elizabeth Barrett   Biographies Pages 596

Gleanings In Genesis (volume I) *by Arthur W. Pink*   ISBN: *1-59462-130-6*   **$27.45**
Appropriately has Genesis been termed "the seed plot of the Bible" for in it we have, in germ form, almost all of the great doctrines which are afterwards fully developed in the books of Scripture which follow...   Religion/Inspirational Pages 420

The Master Key *by L. W. de Laurence*   ISBN: *1-59462-001-6*   **$30.95**
In no branch of human knowledge has there been a more lively increase of the spirit of research during the past few years than in the study of Psychology, Concentration and Mental Discipline. The requests for authentic lessons in Thought Control, Mental Discipline and...   New Age/Business Pages 422

The Lesser Key Of Solomon Goetia *by L. W. de Laurence*   ISBN: *1-59462-092-X*   **$9.95**
This translation of the first book of the "Lernegton" which is now for the first time made accessible to students of Talismanic Magic was done, after careful collation and edition, from numerous Ancient Manuscripts in Hebrew, Latin, and French...   New Age/Occult Pages 92

Rubaiyat Of Omar Khayyam *by Edward Fitzgerald*   ISBN: *1-59462-332-5*   **$13.95**
Edward Fitzgerald, whom the world has already learned, in spite of his own efforts to remain within the shadow of anonymity, to look upon as one of the rarest poets of the century, was born at Bredfield, in Suffolk, on the 31st of March, 1809. He was the third son of John Purcell...   Music Pages 172

Ancient Law *by Henry Maine*   ISBN: *1-59462-128-4*   **$29.95**
The chief object of the following pages is to indicate some of the earliest ideas of mankind, as they are reflected in Ancient Law, and to point out the relation of those ideas to modern thought.   Religion/History Pages 452

Far-Away Stories *by William J. Locke*   ISBN: *1-59462-129-2*   **$19.45**
"Good wine needs no bush, but a collection of mixed vintages does. And this book is just such a collection. Some of the stories I do not want to remain buried for ever in the museum files of dead magazine-numbers an author's not unpardonable vanity..."   Fiction Pages 272

Life of David Crockett *by David Crockett*   ISBN: *1-59462-250-7*   **$27.45**
"Colonel David Crockett was one of the most remarkable men of the times in which he lived. Born in humble life, but gifted with a strong will, an indomitable courage, and unremitting perseverance...   Biographies/New Age Pages 424

Lip-Reading *by Edward Nitchie*   ISBN: *1-59462-206-X*   **$25.95**
Edward B. Nitchie, founder of the New York School for the Hard of Hearing, now the Nitchie School of Lip-Reading, Inc, wrote "LIP-READING Principles and Practice". The development and perfecting of this meritorious work on lip-reading was an undertaking...   How-to Pages 400

A Handbook of Suggestive Therapeutics, Applied Hypnotism, Psychic Science   ISBN: *1-59462-214-0*   **$24.95**
by Henry Munro   Health/New Age/Health/Self-help Pages 376

A Doll's House: and Two Other Plays *by Henrik Ibsen*   ISBN: *1-59462-112-8*   **$19.95**
Henrik Ibsen created this classic when in revolutionary 1848 Rome. Introducing some striking concepts in playwriting for the realist genre, this play has been studied the world over.   Fiction/Classics/Plays 308

The Light of Asia *by sir Edwin Arnold*   ISBN: *1-59462-204-3*   **$13.95**
In this poetic masterpiece, Edwin Arnold describes the life and teachings of Buddha. The man who was to become known as Buddha to the world was born as Prince Gautama of India but he rejected the worldly riches and abandoned the reigns of power when...   Religion/History/Biographies Pages 170

The Complete Works of Guy de Maupassant *by Guy de Maupassant*   ISBN: *1-59462-157-8*   **$16.95**
"For days and days, nights and nights, I had dreamed of that first kiss which was to consecrate our engagement, and I knew not on what spot I should put my lips..."   Fiction/Classics Pages 240

The Art of Cross-Examination *by Francis L. Wellman*   ISBN: *1-59462-309-0*   **$26.95**
Written by a renowned trial lawyer, Wellman imparts his experience and uses case studies to explain how to use psychology to extract desired information through questioning.   How-to/Science/Reference Pages 408

Answered or Unanswered? *by Louisa Vaughan*   ISBN: *1-59462-248-5*   **$10.95**
Miracles of Faith in China   Religion Pages 112

The Edinburgh Lectures on Mental Science (1909) *by Thomas*   ISBN: *1-59462-008-3*   **$11.95**
This book contains the substance of a course of lectures recently given by the writer in the Queen Street Hall, Edinburgh. Its purpose is to indicate the Natural Principles governing the relation between Mental Action and Material Conditions...   New Age/Psychology Pages 148

Ayesha *by H. Rider Haggard*   ISBN: *1-59462-301-5*   **$24.95**
Verily and indeed it is the unexpected that happens! Probably if there was one person upon the earth from whom the Editor of this, and of a certain previous history, did not expect to hear again...   Classics Pages 380

Ayala's Angel *by Anthony Trollope*   ISBN: *1-59462-352-X*   **$29.95**
The two girls were both pretty, but Lucy who was twenty-one who supposed to be simple and comparatively unattractive, whereas Ayala was credited, as her Bombwhat romantic name might show, with poetic charm and a taste for romance. Ayala when her father died was nineteen...   Fiction Pages 484

The American Commonwealth *by James Bryce*   ISBN: *1-59462-286-8*   **$34.45**
An interpretation of American democratic political theory. It examines political mechanics and society from the perspective of Scotsman James Bryce   Politics Pages 572

Stories of the Pilgrims *by Margaret P. Pumphrey*   ISBN: *1-59462-116-0*   **$17.95**
This book explores pilgrims religious oppression in England as well as their escape to Holland and eventual crossing to America on the Mayflower, and their early days in New England...   History Pages 268

QTY

The Fasting Cure *by Sinclair Upton* ISBN: *1-59462-222-1* **$13.95**
In the Cosmopolitan Magazine for May, 1910, and in the Contemporary Review (London) for April, 1910, I published an article dealing with my experi-
ences in fasting. I have written a great many magazine articles, but never one which attracted so much attention... New Age/Self Help/Health Pages 164 ☐

Hebrew Astrology *by Sepharial* ISBN: *1-59462-308-2* **$13.45**
In these days of advanced thinking it is a matter of common observation that we have left many of the old landmarks behind and that we are now pressing
forward to greater heights and to a wider horizon than that which represented the mind-content of our progenitors... Astrology Pages 144 ☐

Thought Vibration or The Law of Attraction in the Thought World ISBN: *1-59462-127-6* **$12.95**

by William Walker Atkinson Psychology/Religion Pages 144 ☐

Optimism *by Helen Keller* ISBN: *1-59462-108-X* **$15.95**
Helen Keller was blind, deaf, and mute since 19 months old, yet famously learned how to overcome these handicaps, communicate with the world, and
spread her lectures promoting optimism. An inspiring read for everyone... Biographies/Inspirational Pages 84 ☐

Sara Crewe *by Frances Burnett* ISBN: *1-59462-360-0* **$9.45**
In the first place, Miss Minchin lived in London. Her home was a large, dull, tall one, in a large, dull square, where all the houses were alike, and all the
sparrows were alike, and where all the door-knockers made the same heavy sound... Childrens/Classic Pages 88 ☐

The Autobiography of Benjamin Franklin *by Benjamin Franklin* ISBN: *1-59462-135-7* **$24.95**
The Autobiography of Benjamin Franklin has probably been more extensively read than any other American historical work, and no other book of its kind
has had such ups and downs of fortune. Franklin lived for many years in England, where he was agent... Biographies/History Pages 332 ☐

Name	
Email	
Telephone	
Address	
City, State ZIP	

☐ **Credit Card**   ☐ **Check / Money Order**

Credit Card Number	
Expiration Date	
Signature	

Please Mail to: *Book Jungle*
PO Box 2226
Champaign, IL 61825
or Fax to: *630-214-0564*

ORDERING INFORMATION

web: *www.bookjungle.com*
email: *sales@bookjungle.com*
fax: *630-214-0564*
mail: *Book Jungle PO Box 2226 Champaign, IL 61825*
or PayPal *to sales@bookjungle.com*

Please contact us for bulk discounts

DIRECT-ORDER TERMS

**20% Discount if You Order
Two or More Books**
Free Domestic Shipping!
Accepted: Master Card, Visa,
Discover, American Express